SPIRIT OF A MOUNTAIN WOLF

Government of South Australia

Asialink

Leaders in Australia–Asia Engagement

The writing of *Mountain Wolf* has been assisted by the
Government of South Australia through Asialink.
This is a work of fiction and, except in the case of historical fact, any
resemblance to actual persons, living or dead, is purely coincidental.
Proceeds from this novel will help in the work of rehabilitating
children who have been trafficked.

SPIRIT OF A MOUNTAIN WOLF

Rosanne Hawke

SCARLET VOYAGE

Scarlet Voyage, an imprint of Enslow Publishers, Inc.

First published in Australia in 2012 under the original title *Mountain Wolf*
by HarperCollins Publishers Australia Pty Limited
ABN 36 009 913 517
harpercollins.com.au

Published by arrangement with Rights People, London

LCCN: 2013943715

Hawke, Rosanne.
     Spirit of a Mountain Wolf / Rosanne Hawke.
     Summary: After Razaq's family is killed in an earthquake, a man preying
on orphans lures Razaq to the city with the promise of finding his uncle.
Instead, Razaq is sold into slavery. Razaq meets Tahira, a young girl suffering
just like him, and hopes to help them both escape before it is too late.

ISBN 978-1-62324-033-2

Future editions:
Paperback ISBN: 978-1-62324-034-9
EPUB ISBN: 978-1-62324-035-6
Single-User PDF ISBN: 978-1-62324-036-3
Multi-User PDF ISBN: 978-1-62324-037-0

Printed in the United States of America

112013 Bang Printing, Brainerd, Minn.

10 9 8 7 6 5 4 3 2 1

Scarlet Voyage
Box 398, 40 Industrial Road
Berkeley Heights, NJ 07922
USA

www.scarletvoyage.com

Cover Illustration: Shutterstock.com

For those children whose lives
have been traded

Chapter 1

Abdur-Razaq Nadeem felt the rumble in the earth—like a truck rushing underground. Then, an eerie heaviness, a sound almost, but there were no words to describe it—like a mourning song with no music. He stood still by the stream, the water in the buckets he held sloshing even though he wasn't moving them. Then the ground roared and shot up beside him as if it were a wave. He fell as another wave rose and his buckets rolled from his hands. This time the stream threw water out at him. He crawled away from the bank, fighting to keep his balance. The ground was a giant blanket shaken in the wind. Razaq reached out to grab a branch, but the tree suddenly disappeared. It was sucked underground in front of him. He backed away, tried to stand, fell again. In the end, he cowered on the ground with his hands over his head as wave after wave of the earth slithered under him and tossed him high.

The roaring had stopped but Razaq couldn't remember when. He looked around; he didn't trust his legs to stand. Boulders from the mountain had landed in the stream, and he was sure the water was flowing in a different direction now. He kneeled and saw a ravine where before there wasn't one. If he had walked just a step, he would have fallen a thousand feet. He vomited on the ground.

He couldn't see the buckets anywhere. His mother would be angry with him. They were the only way to bring water from the stream to the house each morning, and they had cost five rupees in the bazaar in the village down the mountain. It would take him all day to go down for more, if his father had the money.

Razaq began crawling up the slope to his house. The last time the earth had moved, he had been tiny; he remembered the panic, his mother running to pick him up and cradle him beneath her. The roaring had passed quickly that day, and there had been little damage.

After a while, Razaq tested his legs: they felt wobbly but he managed to stagger up the pathway home. When he reached the clearing, he thought he'd lost his way. His house wasn't there. The vegetable plot his mother nurtured had been uprooted. Peepu, their prized ram, lay on the ground. There was something wrong with the way his heavy hoofs stuck out. Razaq ran forward. Peepu was lifeless, his long horns broken. Razaq couldn't see the lambs or the goats. Then he noticed a rock that had fallen from the mountain. A sheep was caught under it. Peepu may have tried to butt the sheep out of the way and the rock had hit him first.

It was then that Razaq realized why he couldn't see the house. He stared at the stones and rocks that covered what had been his mud, stone, and shale home. His mother would have been preparing parathas, his sisters still sleeping. Ramadan had begun, and he and his father had eaten before sunrise.

He stood there, his mind in a mist; he couldn't think what it all meant, didn't dare to.

A charpoy, a string bed, sat the right way up on the ground, as if his father had brought it outside to lie in the sun. Then Razaq heard a groan. He followed the sound onto their terraced farmland.

"Abu!" Razaq could see his father's legs. The trunk of a tree straddled his chest, and his arms were caught under it, too: he must have tried to shield himself. "Abu!" Razaq put two arms around the trunk, straining to shift it, but it didn't budge.

His father opened his eyes. "Alhamdulillah, beta. Praise God, son, you are safe." Razaq had to bend close to hear. "I was worried for you."

"I am fine, Abu ji. I will get help."

"Nay, do not go."

"But, Abu . . ." Razaq sized up the tree. Two men maybe, plus himself, might lift it.

"Listen." His father coughed, then groaned. "Find your Uncle Javaid. Go to Rawalpindi . . ."

"But—"

". . . money in my pocket . . . bus from Oghi . . ."

The breath in his father's throat sounded like a snake's. Razaq had heard that sound before when his grandmother had died.

"Ji, Abu." Razaq kissed his father's face. The sound in his father's throat stopped.

❋

Razaq never found his mother and sisters. He scrabbled at the hill of rock where his house should have been, but without a tool, there was nothing he could do. No one could move a mountain with his hands. He found a branch in the forest and kept picking at the smaller rocks with it, but by nightfall, he was no closer to the house itself. Energy born of shock had carried him through the day, and now it disappeared. He had no sense of how long he sat there keening.

In the night, the roaring came again. He hid behind Peepu. The ground didn't move as badly or open up this time.

In the morning, a man in a black turban with a long beard found him. Razaq hadn't eaten for thirty hours, and he shivered in the morning cold. He eyed the rifle the man held, but saw only peace in his eyes.

"Are there more of your family . . ." The man left the sentence unfinished.

Razaq shook his head faintly.

The man stroked his beard. "A jao, come with me." Then he said, "This is what comes of not submitting to Allah."

The man was his elder, so Razaq didn't say how his father said his prayers and went to the village mosque most Fridays. Razaq had begun to go, too, to join the men. What more did God require? His father always said that to live a good life, to work and look after your family and animals, was submitting to God. Even when Razaq's little brother, Tameem, had died, his father accepted God's will. Still, Razaq knew his father would agree with the man that God had brought the earthquake. Uncle Javaid would have provided some scientific reason. His brother's new thoughts often made Razaq's father argue with him and tell him he was losing his faith. He had told Uncle Javaid last time he was here that the earth was just as flat as the last time they had argued about it.

4

Razaq's breath caught in his throat when he thought of his father. Never again could he ask him anything or climb up the mountain ridge to the forest with him to hunt. And his mother—she kept him working hard, but he'd never thought what it would feel like to not have her calling him, urging him to do his work well, or trying to kiss him, and cuffing him across the head playfully when he refused. He'd give anything to be walking down to the stream with the buckets to get water for the house. If only he had the time over, he'd never do anything grudgingly for his mother again.

"Here." The man indicated the path leading down to the village.

Razaq could see a line of people winding along it toward the Indus River that surged thousands of feet below where the village was. Many—men, women, and children alike—were weeping; others stared ahead as if they could still hear the roar of the earth. He wondered how their neighbours had fared; his friend Ardil's family still lived near them, though Ardil didn't anymore. Halfway down the mountain, Razaq caught sight of the village or what was left of it. The mud and shale buildings were flattened as though a giant had stomped on them. Boulders had rolled into the smaller stream that ran through the village. Bigger stone houses had been cut in half, and Razaq could see the emptiness inside them.

When he reached the village, he saw boats coming from the western tribal area across the Indus. A jeep full of the khan's men roared toward the village on the gravel road, creating a cloud of dust. People huddled in groups near the damaged mosque. Some houses still stood, but people were too frightened to go inside. Most, like Razaq, had no house at all.

The man left Razaq with a group of people, and there, Razaq found Mrs. Daud. It was her daughter, Feeba, who he would marry in a few years, but for now she was still young, only twelve. "Auntie ji?" He found himself clinging to Mrs. Daud as if she were his mother, and he was a young boy. Mrs. Daud burst into sobs.

"Auntie ji . . . ?"

"They are all gone. The children in the madrasah."

Razaq didn't think he could feel anything else, yet his voice sounded strangled when he asked, "Feeba?"

Mrs. Daud spoke and wept at the same time. "She took the boys to the madrasah. She never came home." Her voice rose to a wail when she said "home."

Over Mrs. Daud's head, Razaq watched more jeeps drive into the village and screech to a stop at the madrasah near the mosque. The second story of the madrasah had collapsed onto the floor below. The jeeps were stacked with bags of flour, salt, tea, sugar, and milk. The men took out shovels and picks.

"Excuse me," Razaq said to Mrs. Daud. "I must help."

He felt he had to do something. He couldn't help his own family, but maybe he could help someone else.

A man handed Razaq a shovel, and they set to digging out the rubble. There were dozens of men helping, yet they found only a few boys alive: those who had hidden under the teacher's table. None were Mrs. Daud's sons. There were many dead, and Razaq shifted his mind someplace else so he could work like a buffalo and not think of the bodies they found. Even when Feeba's body was recovered, he could only stare at her. In the distance, he heard the fresh wails of the mothers as they were told of the deaths.

How would they bury them all by nightfall, the required time? The maulvi's son, the priest, called for winding cloths from one of the jeeps. Other men had been digging a long ditch, and the bodies were laid in rows; it looked as if a tribal war had been fought and lost.

Razaq saw the khan by the grave site, leaning on his shovel. Razaq approached him.

"Janab, could some men help me lift a tree off my father so I can bury him?" Razaq averted his eyes in respect as he spoke but tried not to look afraid. Everyone knew khans could be moody and might order you killed if they decided you deserved it. But the thought of his father alone on the mountain at the mercy of wild dogs had haunted him all morning, and he kept his chin high.

Something flickered in the khan's eyes as he looked at Razaq's face. Then he called to two older boys. "Hussain, Abdul, go with him. Take your shovels." The order came with a movement of his head and hand.

The boys slung their AK-47s over their shoulders and joined Razaq. He was so tired he felt like dropping to the ground to sleep, but he had to bury his father. As they began to ascend the pathway up the mountain, he looked back to find the khan staring after him.

"Did you lose many in your family?" the shorter boy, Hussain, asked as they walked with slow, long strides.

"All." Razaq's tone was terse.

"You should come with us then, shouldn't he, Abdul?"

Razaq glanced at him. "Why?"

"We are being trained to fight. We keep the mountains safe from militants."

"Don't you have a family?" Razaq asked.

"In Swat, I have a family," Abdul said. "I miss them, but this is good work. One day, I shall make some money and send it back to them."

"I don't want to fight," Razaq said.

All he wanted right then was to do what his father had done, and his father before him: live on the mountain in peace, keep sheep and goats, and grow corn. Marry Feeba, too. He squeezed his eyes shut as the images from the madrasah finally brought the tears.

Hussain and Abdul strode behind him. It wasn't unusual to see men cry openly when someone they loved died.

❈

The boys grunted and strained as they used the shovels as levers to pry up the tree and roll it off Razaq's father. Razaq hesitated when he saw his father's injuries.

"Come," Hussain said. "We must dig."

For the next hour, Razaq had no energy to think about what his father had suffered. It was a mercy the ground was soft. They laid his father inside the earth. The boys waited while Razaq checked his father's pockets and found the purse. He took the tarveez from his father's neck and tied it around his own; he gently unbuckled the sandals from his father's feet and put them on. Then they covered him. Razaq brought rocks and laid them on top. *That should stop the jackals.* He stood and stared at the grave. This was the land his father had worked; now it was his portion. Could he build another house? It seemed too difficult a task.

He thought of the words that were said when baby Tameem died. "Allahu Akbar, God is great," he murmured.

They heard a wild dog howl.

"We must go," Abdul said with a quick glance up the mountain. "It is getting late."

The moon was high when the boys reached the village. Razaq thanked them and sought out Mrs. Daud. She was still awake, laying blankets over plastic on the ground. Her face was tear streaked, and her hair had fallen down. He felt sorry for her: she had lost everyone as he had, but she had rarely gone out of the house, and here she must feel so exposed.

"I was given some chapattis, beta," she said when she saw him. "Here, I kept two for you."

She handed them to him in a daze. Razaq wasn't even sure if she knew who he was.

He lay on the ground nearby, wrapped a blanket around himself, and put some chapatti in his pocket to eat in the morning before the fast began. He wished he had his shawl his mother had woven for him. It was much warmer than the blanket.

During the night, a man walked by and lingered near Mrs. Daud. Razaq sat up and the man moved on. He decided then he would stay with her: she needed him, just as his mother would have.

Chapter 2

The next day, two things happened: an army truck trundled into the village, and in its wake came a jeep of aid workers. The villagers called them Angrez. Razaq heard some men saying the Angrez shouldn't be there, that they would have to leave. Both groups gave out tents. Razaq stood in line at the army truck, but there was much pushing and shoving. Twice Razaq fell out of line—he was not big enough to fight a grown man, and besides, he had been taught to respect his elders. To see men acting like this troubled him. Some men took two tents. Finally, by persistence alone, Razaq managed to get one for Mrs. Daud. With it came a saucepan, a spoon, and two tin cups.

Mrs. Daud gave him a small smile when she saw the tent. "I did not want to sleep in the cold again. You are a good boy and young enough to sleep in it with me."

Razaq thought he probably wasn't, but his lack of mustache made him seem younger. He recalled how Uncle Javaid had shaved his beard off on purpose. "Men in the cities do that," he had said to Razaq after another argument with Razaq's father.

The Angrez had set up some tents and were giving out food packages. Most of the tribal men were fighting for flour near the army truck. A soldier stood by with a rifle cocked, shouting at them to form a line. Razaq had never seen mountain men stand in a line and didn't think much of the soldier's chances of succeeding. Very few men had gone near the Angrez, and Razaq decided to see what was happening at their tents.

First, he saw a woman, younger than his mother, but with strange reddish-brown hair as if she had put henna in it. Her shawl kept falling off her head. Even Layla, his youngest sister, could keep a shawl on. The woman smiled at him, but he didn't smile in return. He was definitely too old to be smiling at young women; her husband may beat him. He'd seen a man kill a stranger for speaking to his wife.

The woman said something, but he didn't understand. A white-skinned man joined her, and Razaq stiffened. Would he think he had been talking to the woman? She said the strange words to the man, and he turned to Razaq and smiled as well. This time Razaq allowed a tentative smile back.

"You are welcome," the man said in Urdu. "We have programs for young people like you since you have lost your school. Come tomorrow—we will teach you Angrezi, English. It will help you get a job."

Razaq took more notice when he heard the word "job," though he didn't think much of the rest of what the man had said. How young did they think he was? He hadn't been to the madrasah since he was twelve, and even then his attendance was sporadic. He checked the animals, milked the goats, and only then went to the madrasah if he had time. He used to memorize his verses while he was working; if he got them wrong the teacher would beat him with a stick. The old teacher always called him by his full name: Abdur-

Razaq. It was as if he thought it a sin to shorten it to Razaq as his family had done.

"Here's some food for today." The Angrez man gave him a small bag of flour and some salt and tea. "Small bags are best," he said, "then no one will notice."

Razaq wondered what he meant until he saw a man beaten up on the path and his big army bag of flour snatched. He managed to deliver the food to Mrs. Daud intact. She was weeping again and still hadn't started a fire, so Razaq went to find wood. When he returned, Mrs. Daud sniffed.

"If my husband were here . . ." She broke off, then said, "But you are here now, beta, thank you."

Razaq was uncomfortable with her calling him her son. Older women often called boys his age "beta," but Mrs. Daud sounded as though she truly believed he was her son. What if he needed to return to his land and rebuild the house? Would she let him go?

❋

That day, Razaq's time was spent collecting wood, bringing water from the river, and jostling in lines for more food. The army didn't stay but appointed an elder in the village to administer the food they had brought. Razaq found it had been easier to get food at the Angrez tents, even though he knew many of the men distrusted them.

The following day, he ignored the Angrez man's invitation to learn English and helped search for bodies instead. The local khan estimated more than half of the people in the village and surrounding tribal areas had died in the earthquake. Since the maulvi had also died, his son, Wazir Ahmad, led the prayers outside the mosque. Although the building still stood, it was deemed too dangerous to use because of the aftershocks.

"Almost everyone died in Balakot," Wazir Ahmad said. "Allah be praised not all of us have died here, but winter is coming soon. We must help each other to rebuild."

"But how?" one man called out. "We have no materials, no money."

"We can use the stone from the broken houses," another man said.

"If you have a stone house. Mine was mud."

"Kharmosh, quiet," Wazir Ahmad said. "The government is sending supplies and money. The tribal leaders have asked for aid."

There were grumblings. Razaq knew why. His father, like all tribal men, had put no hope in the government. The khans didn't want militants in their tribal area; they governed their lands themselves with jirgas, local councils. Would the government help people who did not recognize the government's power? Razaq thought not. The army truck had only stayed a day; the soldiers hadn't ventured into the mountains to check if anyone was still alive up there, and they hadn't left enough tents.

That night, Razaq woke to the sound of stealthy footsteps around their tent. He heard the sound of a tent peg being pulled. He shot up from his blanket, grabbed the shovel, and burst outside. Two men were in the act of dismantling the tent.

"Have you no shame?" Razaq cried. "A widow lives here."

"We are cold," said one, but the other punched Razaq in the face. Razaq staggered, but he still had hold of the shovel. He lifted it just as the man tried to hit him again.

The man's hand struck the shovel instead. He grunted. "You little shaitan."

Razaq aimed the shovel as if he'd strike him with it. "Leave us alone."

Two more men appeared behind the attackers. Razaq's heart sank. He couldn't fight off four of them. Then one of the newcomers spoke. "Having trouble, Razaq?"

It was Hussain and Abdul. They held their guns casually in their hands, and the two thieves quickly disappeared.

Hussain eyed the shovel. "You should learn to fight properly. You need a gun."

Razaq thought of his prized rifle: a British Lee Enfield .303—more expensive than the boys' AK-47s—with two yellow stripes and flowers painted around the butt. It had been his grandfather's, and now it was under a hill of stones along with his mother and sisters.

"You will make a good fighter," Hussain said. "The government wants to rule our lands—do you want that?"

Razaq shook his head, but his heart wasn't in it. He didn't wish to fight unless it was to protect his sheep and goats and Peepu. Then he thought of Mrs. Daud and managed to grin at his new friends. "Thank you for coming. Now Mrs. Daud still has her tent."

❈

Razaq knew he would need a job to get food for Mrs. Daud. He couldn't see any goats around to mind—they must have drowned in the river. It would be good if he could have a ram of his own, but they were expensive; it had taken his father most of his life selling goats to raise the money to buy Peepu, the special ram he was using to build up their own herd. Thoughts of Peepu and his family always made Razaq stop still even if he was walking. Would the image of his father dead on the ground ever fade from his mind? He pushed it aside and thought of Mrs. Daud instead. She didn't have any money, and he didn't want to use his father's purse if he could help it. Maybe he would find his uncle later on, though minibuses to Rawalpindi or Peshawar were expensive. But he couldn't leave Mrs. Daud yet. He thought again of the Angrez and their offer. They'd talked about English lessons; he would see what they meant.

When he returned to the tents set up by the Angrez, a village man was stringing up a green banner. Razaq couldn't read it but the man saw him staring. "It means you have a right to play. It is Angrezi."

Razaq frowned; when had he last played unless he was minding his sisters, but even then they were looking after the goats. "Play?" he said aloud.

"Ji. The Angrez are crazy—their children do not work, and they stay babies all their lives."

"Truly?" Razaq could not imagine a family where the children didn't work. "They must have much money."

The man spat. "The Angrez are filthy rich." Then he added, "They will not last here—the tribals do not accept them. And the woman is bad—why is she not wearing a burqa?"

Razaq's mother always wore a burqa if she went out, but she hardly ever left the house—only if a friend had a baby or there was a wedding.

The man continued his tirade. "That man isn't her husband or brother, and why did her father let her come by herself? See, even he has washed his hands of her. If women are not daughters, mothers, sisters, or wives, they are gashtian, whores."

Razaq stared at him in shock. He'd heard of whores. He knew it was haram for a woman to do bura kam, bad work like that, but once his mother had told him that a woman would do anything for her children, even sell herself if she had nothing, just to feed them. He imagined his mother doing anything for him and his sisters; not that she'd sell herself, but when the roaring came she would have gathered his sisters and covered them with her body, as she had done with him when he was little. But this time a rock had fallen off the mountain. He closed his eyes. Perhaps he hadn't tried hard enough. What if they had been still alive like those boys under the teacher's table?

"All Angrez women are gashtian," the man was saying. "I have been to Peshawar and seen the Internet. You should see what they do for money."

Razaq didn't know what an Internet was, but he knew he was tired of listening to this man's evil talk. "Why are you helping them then?" he asked.

"They are paying me. I need a job."

So do I, thought Razaq and pulled aside the flap of the tent.

"Ao, come." The henna-haired woman had learned an Urdu word. She gestured to him in the way he would call a dog, then he realized she didn't know it was offensive. He walked toward her, the village man's words ringing in his ears. She didn't look poor enough to become a whore.

"My name—Rebekah," she said, proud of her new words, but they sounded strange.

The Angrez man smiled too. "I'm Karl. I'm from Australia, and Rebekah is from Canada. We came to help." His Urdu was easier to understand.

Razaq saw Pakistani people in the tent, but they were not from the mountains: they had darker skin. One woman was teaching a few girls, which Razaq thought odd. Karl took him to another tent where a man was teaching boys. They were having an English lesson. The boys didn't look as old as he was, and Razaq hesitated.

Karl said, "You can sit in the back. Later you can help the teacher. If you do this as a job we can give you food."

That made up Razaq's mind. He was sick of standing in food lines for hours to get a few potatoes. It made him feel useless that he couldn't do a day's work, and then there were the fights. He sat on the floor behind the other boys.

"Say it again," the teacher said. "How are you?"

All the boys chorused, "How are you, Mr. Harish?"

"I am fine," the teacher said.

"I am fine," copied the boys.

Razaq found himself joining in. It would impress his uncle if he could speak Angrezi. Uncle Javaid had told Razaq's father that Razaq should go to the city and stay with him and Amina so he could go to school to learn English and math. But Razaq's father didn't agree. He hadn't even gone to the madrasah; it was Uncle Javaid who had attended and look what it did for him. Razaq's father had said: "It took him away from the mountains." He had said to always stay in the mountains, so Razaq found it confusing that his father had told him to find his uncle. Had it been death talking or should he act on his father's last wish?

At the end of the lesson, Mr. Harish asked Razaq to help him. "The younger boys need to play soccer—to have a time of forgetting."

Razaq nodded. He didn't know how to play, though his uncle had given him a ball once. He'd kicked it around until his father told him it might frighten the goats.

Mr. Harish divided the boys into two teams. "You take that team," he said to Razaq. "Just tell them to keep their eye on the ball, and break up any fights."

Razaq watched Mr. Harish carefully and did everything the same. "Kick the ball," he shouted after he'd heard Mr. Harish say it. Razaq even got to kick it himself. Mr. Harish was right: when he and the boys were running after that ball, it was all he could think of. His mind wasn't filled with images of his bloodied father, of Peepu and his broken horns, his responsibility for Mrs. Daud, and whether he should find his uncle. He just heard the singing of the wind in his ears.

After the game, he grinned at Mr. Harish. "Accha hai."

"Can you say it in English?"

"It is good," Razaq said.

Mr. Harish laid his hand on Razaq's head. "I am glad for that," he said, and Razaq recognized the concern in his eyes.

Being at the Angrez tents made Razaq feel almost carefree, and he went again in the afternoon. Mrs. Daud didn't seem to care or even understand where he went as long as he brought food. His father would have said to be careful of Angrez people—they were immoral and worshipped three gods—but Karl had told Razaq he worshipped one god, too, so Razaq knew he must be Muslim.

That evening, after another exhilarating game of soccer, a man approached Razaq. "I saw you playing soccer," he said. "You're very good."

The man was his uncle's age, dressed in a clean shalwar qameez, and Razaq stood still in respect.

"You could get a job in the city playing soccer."

Razaq grinned. The man was joking.

"No, it's true. Haven't you seen games on TV?"

Razaq stayed silent. He had never seen TV, though he'd heard of it, nor did he know what the man's business was. Men did not stop you on the path to talk about nothing. They visited your father and drank tea and . . . Razaq sighed inwardly. From now on, he had to work things out, make decisions, himself.

"I could take you to the city. Do you know anyone in Rawalpindi?"

Razaq looked at the man with more interest. "My uncle lives there."

"I might be able to take you to him and get you a job. What can you do here?" The man lifted his arm to encompass the broken village.

Razaq bit his lip. He needed a job, but there was Mrs. Daud. He couldn't leave her yet—she still didn't remember who he was.

"I will think about this," Razaq said politely and moved on.

When he glanced back, the man had taken out a cigarette, and he blew smoke in his direction. Razaq knew then the man wasn't a good Muslim: no one was supposed to smoke during the Ramadan fast.

Chapter 3

Razaq continued to help in the Angrez tents. He scrutinized Rebekah, even looked in her eyes, for signs of whoring, but all he saw was the way his mother or Mrs. Daud had looked at him before the earthquake. Rebekah looked at him as if she wanted to adopt him. Wouldn't a gashtee look at you differently, make you feel something that a wife should make you feel?

He'd decided in the night not to go to Rawalpindi yet. He may need to stay until a house could be built for Mrs. Daud, or at least until her brother could come to claim her. But not all brothers wanted a widowed sister to feed forever. It was too much to think of right now, and he was being paid by the Angrez in food and clothes for his help with the younger boys. It was enough. So he was troubled to arrive back at Mrs. Daud's tent to find the man who had stopped him on the road sitting outside talking to her. She had her shawl over her face. Poor Mrs. Daud—she had always worn a burqa if she ever ventured outside, but it must have disappeared with her house.

"Ah, here he is," the man said when he saw Razaq.

"Assalamu alaikum." Razaq said it slowly. The man must have followed him home yesterday. What could he want? Should he stay with Mrs. Daud during the day as well?

Mrs. Daud smiled at him. "Mr. Ikram has a good proposition for you, beta."

Razaq stood looking at her.

"Sit down, beta." She motioned to the mat beside her. She was stirring chai in the saucepan over the fire. She wouldn't have any herself since the fast hadn't yet broken for the day; she must be making it for the guest.

The man Ikram spoke. "I've been telling your mother about taking you to the city. A good-looking boy like you can get a job and send money back to her."

Razaq waited for Mrs. Daud to say he wasn't her son, but she kept stirring the chai.

"What do you say, sahiba?" Ikram asked.

Mrs. Daud smiled to be addressed as a lady. "It is a good idea."

"There is nothing here for him, is there?" Ikram said.

"But I bring her food," Razaq cut in. When was she going to say she needed him? "How will she get that herself in the lines? The men with families always push in first."

Mrs. Daud turned to him. "He will give me money." Then she smiled again. "Lots of it—three hundred rupees."

Razaq was shocked into silence. It was obviously more money than she had ever seen, but it wouldn't help her build a house. The food was free at the moment, but it wouldn't always be so and the prices would rise. And what if he didn't get a job straight away?

"That won't last long," he said eventually.

It was as if Ikram could read his thoughts. "I know where you can get a job immediately," he said. "Then you can start sending money home. You can find your uncle later."

"It is very generous, beta," Mrs. Daud said. "He need not give me anything at all."

Razaq frowned. He wasn't sure he wanted to go yet, and why should he go with Ikram? "I can go by myself when I am ready," he said.

"But I know where the job is," Ikram said.

Razaq thought he sounded irritated. Then Ikram reached for his money and held it out to Mrs. Daud. Razaq stared at it resting on Ikram's palm. As soon as Mrs. Daud took it, his destiny would be sealed.

"Think about this more," Razaq implored her.

"I have thought enough." She reached for the money. "You need to make your own way, beta."

Even in that moment he wasn't sure what meaning she put on the word *beta*. Did she still think he was her son? He wished he could talk about this in private with her—she wasn't thinking carefully. Had she considered what the nights would be like without him? How would she fight off tent stealers? He had a squirmy feeling in his gut. He stared at the money in her hands as she counted it. Yes, it was generous of the man, but for some reason, he felt bought.

"We should go now," Ikram said.

"Now? Can't I say good-bye to my friends?"

"A jeep is leaving in a few minutes to take us to the bus. We cannot miss it—there are so few buses running up here at the moment. Get your things."

Ikram's voice had a sudden ring of authority, and Razaq frowned as he went into the tent. He already had on his father's sandals, his knitted vest, jacket, and his pakol, his lambswool hat. He slipped the purse with its one hundred and twenty rupees into his pocket and bundled a shalwar qameez that Karl had given him into a plastic bag. When he emerged, Ikram stood up.

"It is a great tragedy here, but I am glad I can help one boy find a future."

Mrs. Daud smiled at Ikram. It was the happiest Razaq had seen her since the earthquake.

He didn't even have time to tell Abdul and Hussain to keep an eye out for Mrs. Daud, or to thank Rebekah, Karl, and Mr. Harish for their kindness. He was practically shoved into the jeep and was soon tearing alongside the Indus River. When he looked back at the mountains, he couldn't even see where his home had been.

❋

When they climbed onto the minibus at Oghi, Ikram spoke to the driver as if he knew him. Razaq didn't see Ikram buy a ticket, and he didn't feel like pulling out his father's purse to offer. None of this was his idea; let Ikram pay for him. His only consoling thought was that his father had wanted him to do this, too, and it calmed him a little.

The bus driver stared at Razaq and winked at Ikram. "Got a good-looker there, yar."

Ikram laughed while Razaq scowled and wondered what his looks had to do with anything. His mother said he was a handsome boy, and even though he wasn't as tall as others his age, she said he soon would be. She always told him to look at a man's deeds not how tall he was, but all mothers said things like that.

They sat at the back of the bus, where one man touched Razaq on the cheek and another let his hand rest on his leg. "Khubsurat baccha, beautiful child."

"Chup, be quiet," Ikram said, slapping the man's hand away. "He's my nephew."

The other men laughed. "How many nephews do you have, Ikram sahib?"

An old man told them all to shut their mouths. "Shame on you, it is Ramadan. And have a thought for the suffering of the mountain people."

One young man muttered, "That is why I am leaving."

Razaq had never been in a bus, and his eyes kept straying to the colorful transfers on the windscreen. One was of a black horse in full gallop. There was something like a tarveez hanging from the driver's mirror. Razaq touched his father's tarveez under his shirt. He hoped it would protect him better than it had his father, and then instantly felt sorry for thinking such a disloyal thing. The engine revved and the bus drew out of the adda, the terminal. Once it was on the Karakoram Highway, it picked up speed. The tarveez on the mirror swayed every time the bus swerved to miss rocks and potholes. Razaq hoped it was strong enough to protect them from accidents. His gaze slid again to the horse on the window. Would it be like this to ride a horse, he wondered. He had never traveled so fast. At times, his stomach felt as though he had left it back at Oghi.

At one point, they had to wait while a bulldozer shifted rocks off the road. Razaq relieved himself by the verge. When he stood up, tying his narda, his shalwar cord, he found the bus driver close behind him.

"Is there any problem?" Razaq asked. The bus driver shrugged his shoulders and gave a sideways glance at Ikram who was smoking nearby. Razaq had the odd feeling Ikram was keeping an eye on him.

It was midnight when they arrived at a bus adda in Rawalpindi. As they stepped off the bus, the driver said something to Ikram that Razaq didn't catch. Ikram shook his head and said, "Sorry, Saleem."

Razaq hadn't felt this tired even after the burial of his father. Dust filled his nose and eyes, and the smell of fumes was stifling. It was warmer than the mountains, but Razaq couldn't see the stars; there was too much light from the street. Even this late, buses were coming and going, conductors calling out their destinations.

Ikram took him to a small restaurant in the terminal, a little bigger than a booth. Wooden tables and benches stood outside. Inside, there were a few more tables and a TV set switched on for the customers. Razaq couldn't take his eyes off the people on the screen. A woman was crying, but he knew it wasn't real, just a play. So this was what Uncle Javaid had described to him.

Ikram ordered chai and dhal for them both. Razaq was hungry; truly he had fasted long today even though travelers didn't have to. When the dhal came, Ikram called the owner from the kitchen.

"Janab," Ikram said to him, lifting his chin. "Look who I have here." He said to Razaq, "Look up, boy. Say salaam to Mr. Kazim."

Razaq lifted his head from his dhal, and Kazim drew in a breath. His eyes glistened as he pulled his gaze away from Razaq back to Ikram. "Where did you find him?"

"Kala Dhaka, Black Mountain. They were hit but not as badly as Balakot.

They're still feudal up there, six hundred years behind the rest of us."

"Incredible." Kazim's gaze kept returning to Razaq, who ducked his head in embarrassment to take a mouthful of dhal. "So this is what those tribals look like. Those eyes—so beautiful and innocent." He glanced quickly at Ikram. "He is untouched?"

Ikram nodded. "He's the genuine article. His name is Razaq. You interested?"

Razaq saw the look of a bargainer slide across Kazim's face. "You must realize I have many expenses."

Ikram grunted. "In this poky hole?" Then he leaned forward. "Ten thousand rupees."

Kazim put a pained look on his face. Razaq watched in fascination. The previous owner of Peepu had that same expression when Razaq's father was buying him. "I do not have that much. One thousand rupees."

Ikram chuckled. "You shame me."

"Two thousand then."

"Nine thousand, five hundred." Ikram's eyes glinted like steel.

"Two thousand, five hundred."

Razaq sat straighter. He was so tired it was hard to tell, but was he being sold? How could that be? He was a person, not a ram. You couldn't sell people. Maybe it was a joke. When friends got together there was much joking, like on the bus. He waited to see.

"Eight thousand," Ikram's voice fired like a gun going off.

"Three thousand."

"Seven thousand, five hundred."

"Three thousand, five hundred."

"Six thousand, not a rupee less, Kazim."

"You will ruin me."

"But you can afford it, you old rogue. The money now, or I'll take him to Saleem. He'll pay more."

Kazim disappeared into the other room.

"What are you doing?" Razaq asked.

Ikram regarded him a moment, then he said, "This is your job."

"But why does he have to pay you?"

"It's my commission for finding you. You will work for him, and soon you can send money home to your mother. Lots of boys from the mountains have jobs like this in the city."

Razaq looked around the dingy restaurant. He had thought of looking after someone's animals—he knew how to do that. Cooking—could he cook? He could learn, he supposed. He nodded slowly. He was too tired to look for another job. If he didn't like this one, he could look for a different one next week. Then he could find his uncle.

Kazim came back and handed Ikram a wad of notes.

"Keeping so much cash here," Ikram said as he counted it. "Aren't you afraid of being robbed, old man?"

"You just robbed me," Kazim said darkly.

Ikram stood up. "But you need him. Didn't you just lose a boy?" Then he turned to Razaq. "Work hard and you'll stay alive."

Razaq watched him leave, wondering why he'd say such a strange thing.

"Chello, get a move on, boy. You may as well start earning your keep," Kazim said.

He took Razaq into the other room. There was a double gas burner with two large pots heating and two plastic bowls on a wooden table. There was a trough with taps and buckets of water underneath. Razaq had only seen a trough like that at the mosque in the village.

"Boil up some water in the kettle and wash these chai cups," Kazim said. "My nephew has gone home for the night. You can be the night shift."

Razaq had never seen a kettle and Kazim had to show him how to switch it on. "Electricity," Kazim said too loudly. Razaq nodded; he'd heard about electricity.

He could barely keep his eyes open, but he managed to wash dishes for two hours while Kazim came in and out to make chai and heat up curry for customers.

"Tomorrow night you can do this, too," he said, "and run for bread from the local naan shop."

Razaq could hear the noise of the bus station through the thin wooden walls, but as time passed, it seemed to lessen. He wasn't sure if it was because he was so tired his ears weren't working properly or if there were fewer buses running.

Finally, Kazim came back in. "You can sleep now. It is three o'clock in the morning. Tomorrow night you will work until five when my nephew Aslam starts."

He showed Razaq a blanket in the corner. It looked like a dog's bed, but right then Razaq could have slept on stones. He put his bundle between him and the wooden wall and fell on the blanket. He didn't even remember landing.

Chapter 4

Javaid Khan was at work in the Fazal Clothing Emporium when the earthquake struck. The shock rumbled all the way down Moti Bazaar, and customers dropped the cloth they were holding and rushed out to Iqbal Road. There was little damage, and after a few hours, the customers returned to start their bargaining all over again. Javaid had not felt the freedom to flee the shop, but he had locked the till for he knew as well as Waqar, his boss, that some would take advantage of an earthquake to pilfer from shops. When the danger was past and the electricity was back on, he listened to the news on the TV Waqar kept in the shop. Both Waqar and Javaid were cricket fanatics, and the TV was usually on for customers to see the progress of a match while they shopped. Many men brought their women to buy cloth, and during cricket telecasts, Waqar's shop drew the most customers.

Javaid heard how the epicenter of the earthquake had hit the tribal areas in the mountains, in Balakot and Azad Kashmir. Thousands dead, the news reporter said. The town of Balakot was decimated with few survivors. *That's fifty thousand dead alone,* Javaid thought. Kohistan and Kala Dhaka were affected but not as badly. At least there were survivors in Kala Dhaka, though no one knew how many: the tribal areas were closed.

"Let them bury their own dead up there," a customer muttered.

Javaid watched the news in shock. What of Nadeem and his family? He should go and help. Waqar was watching over his shoulder. When Javaid looked up, Waqar inclined his head in sympathy.

"I have to go," Javaid said.

Waqar hesitated. "What can you do?"

"I can see if my family is alive. Then I'll come back. Please, give me a week. Someone may have died."

Waqar shrugged. Always he was losing staff to attend weddings or funerals. Death was a familiar companion and the burial rites had to be observed. "I need you to finish the accounts first," he said, then walked off before Javaid could argue.

Every day, Javaid watched the news, but there was little said about the tribal areas. The reports were full of Azad Kashmir. In his lunch hour, he googled Kala Dhaka. There were no updates of the earthquake, but he found images that brought tears to his eyes: the twenty-mile mountain range that rose straight up from the Indus; mountain fields he used to roam in as a boy with Nadeem, thick with flowers and fresh air; a tourist's travel photos of the villages, the ruins of the old British fort on a ridge top. He had explored that as a boy, too. How much of Kala Dhaka was left?

It took him four days to bring the books up to date. Although Waqar was a hard businessman, it wasn't like him to be so unreasonable, but no one else could use the software on the computer, and who knew how long Javaid would be or whether he would even return? On the next day, Javaid asked again. He feared Waqar would think of some other excuse, but this time he merely sighed. "Jao, go," he said.

That afternoon, Amina met Javaid at the door of their two-roomed mud house in the Badi Mohalla behind Raja Bazaar. He parked his bicycle in their tiny courtyard.

"Have you heard from home today?" she asked.

"No, but I have a chutti at last to go up there."

She laid a hand on his arm. "Do not worry, your family would have survived. My Auntie Latifa and her family, too." She reached up to touch his cheek. "It is far enough from Balakot."

Javaid gave a heavy sigh. "It's only thirty miles across the mountains."

Just then, a little girl flew into his arms. "Abu ji, you are home early. You have a surprise?"

Javaid smiled at her and pulled a bubblegum from his pocket.

"Yum, Hubba Bubba, my favorite."

Javaid hugged her tightly. *Thank God she was safe.*

"Abu?" the little girl said.

"Ji, Sakina?"

"Are you happy?" Her little face puckered around her eyes.

"Ji beti, I am happy. I have you to love." Then he turned to Amina. "I'll leave tonight, take a bus north."

❋

Javaid took a rickshaw to a bus terminal on the Grand Trunk Road. It was 8:00 P.M. He bought a ticket and drank a cup of chai at a kacha, or makeshift, restaurant while he waited. He glanced around at the grimy wooden walls, the fly spots on the table, and shrugged. Most people were poor and did the best they could, he knew. So many like himself came from rural areas to make a living in the city, to have a better future for their families. He had been more fortunate than most: his talents in math and computers meant he was truly the one who ran the business of the Fazal Clothing Emporium. He smiled to himself; it was a fancy name for what was really only a shop, but Waqar's grandfather had named it that after the Partition. Now Amina didn't have to slave with animals like her mother had, and Sakina could go to school. Education for girls was accepted in the city. Maybe when he had enough money, he could start a school for girls in the mountains. But would anyone use it? He knew his brother's view on educating girls: "It will only cause trouble. They will think they know more than men and get argumentative."

Javaid clenched his fingers around the chipped cup. These thoughts made him wish the bus would hurry up and leave. How badly had Kala Dhaka been hit? There was no accurate news.

He heard a boy call a destination: "Oghi, Oghi, Oghi." Javaid pushed away the cup, picked up his backpack, and boarded the bus. He sat near the front; he knew from experience that the rear of the bus was bumpy enough to put his spine out of line.

Once they reached Abbottabad, the journey to Oghi took twice as long as usual due to a fresh landslide. After a harrowing jeep ride along a potholed bitumen road into the tribal areas, Javaid finally reached Kala Dhaka the next day. He stopped at the village above the river where the mountain people got many of their supplies. It was early morning and bitterly cold. He wrapped his goat's hair shawl around himself, a gift from his mother before she died. He felt a twinge of guilt: he should have come home more often. Little Tameem's funeral was the last time, almost a year ago. His mother's funeral the time before that. Was it only death and marriages that brought him home?

"God willing, let it not be death this time," he murmured.

He shouldered his backpack and made his way to the mosque and madrasah. He had gone to the madrasah as a boy and not many of his memories were good. It wasn't where he had learned his math, English, and computing. He'd taken night classes for those in the city.

Javaid was met by a pile of rubble where once the madrasah had stood—rock, cement, and wood all tumbled together like rubbish. A sickening feeling uncurled in his gut. Razaq would be fourteen, too old for the madrasah, wouldn't he?

He raced across to the mosque. It looked abandoned. He stopped a man carrying food in plastic bags. "Excuse me, where is the maulvi?"

"The maulvi died," the man said. "A wall fell on him."

Javaid walked around the village in a daze. Some of the better-built houses still stood, though they were damaged, but there was no life inside. Then there were the piles of rubble that had once been houses. One of these was the home of Amina's Auntie Latifa.

He couldn't put off going up the mountain any longer. He had to make sure his family was safe. The long walk up the near vertical path tired him out, as it always did when he visited. He'd become accustomed to the thicker air of the plains. When he was younger, he had run up this path. Every time he glanced down at the Indus it grew smaller, until it looked like a light blue ribbon lying at the foot of the mountain.

When he finally reached Nadeem's land, a wave of nausea washed over him. The house was gone—there was just a pile of stones and mud with a huge rock perched on top like some prehistoric predator. The house had been dry-stacked stone with mud plaster and a wooden frame; it wouldn't have taken much to destroy it.

He could smell the carcass of the ram from ten paces, and saw that the birds and wild dogs had been busy. How the children had loved that animal. Razaq had even made a leather bridle for it.

He wandered onto the terraced farmland and found the grave under the trees. He kneeled beside it. Whose was it? It was new and, in Muslim fashion, had no marker. It was an adult grave: Nadeem's or Zarina's? He wished he could find out, but nothing would induce him to desecrate a grave. A family member must have dug it, so surely someone in his family was alive.

He sat by the grave for an hour, then said his prayers. He walked across to the pile of rubble that had been the house. Had they run out as soon as they felt the earth trembling? He sat on Nadeem's charpoy and stared at the scene before him. Something glinted in the sunlight filtering through the trees, something red near the rubble. When he rose to check, he found it was red glass, a tiny broken bangle. That was when the tears finally came. He sank to his knees in the stones and wept like a child.

Chapter 5

Razaq was woken in the morning by a thumping sound. He opened one eye to see a boy a little younger than himself squatting on the ground and grinding spices by banging a wooden pestle into a narrow wooden bowl. His mother used a wooden pestle like that to crush coriander seeds, cumin, and cardamom. She crushed ginger and garlic in it, too. Razaq rolled over and groaned. His back felt like he had been roped between two buffaloes turning a waterwheel in opposite directions.

The other boy turned; this must be Aslam. "So you wake at last. It is midday." He was pinched in the face with a haunted look. Razaq thought his eyes were those of a hunted wolf in the forest. The boy glanced nervously out to the eating area. "You had better get some naan soon."

Razaq went outside to pee in a drain. The smells of the curry the other boy was cooking made his stomach rumble. When he came back in, the boy gave him a chapatti and a bowl of leftover curry. In it was floating one piece of bone with a few tufts of meat clinging to it. It had more chili than Razaq was used to, but he guessed it was all he would get. He pushed it down while Aslam told him where to go to buy the bread for customers.

He raced out, dodged buses, dogs, bicycles, and travelers with their bags. The boy cooking the naan at the tandoor oven was older than he was, more like Hussain's age. "Haven't seen you before," he said. "You new around here?"

Razaq nodded. "I work for Kazim."

The boy didn't reply at first; he was concentrating on getting the bread out of the clay tandoor with his long hooked rod. "Kazim with the teashop?" he finally asked.

"It is called a restaurant," Razaq said.

"I suppose that's possible," said the boy as he wrapped the bread in newspaper. "Watch your back, that's all I can say."

The warm smell of the risen bread made Razaq feel hungry. He had only eaten naan a few times at weddings in the village. It had been very tasty as he remembered. Next time, he would take some of his father's money and buy himself one. Maybe it wouldn't matter that it was Ramadan—the bus terminal seemed to be exempt from the fast: he could see men eating as they walked to the buses.

Back in the kitchen, he checked Aslam wasn't watching and took out his father's purse. He fingered the paper notes. He had never had money of his own. Sometimes they swapped milk for eggs with Ardil's family if the chickens weren't laying, or apricots for grapes, but there was never an exchange of money. His father grew small crops of rice and wheat or corn. They had only just harvested the corn before the earthquake, and they hadn't yet separated their own needs from what they would give to the khan. It had all been lost. And Peepu, the animals. He tried to keep his mind away from his mother and sisters, the image of his father's body. He put five rupees in his pocket, then he hid the purse under his blanket.

The second time that day he was sent to the tandoor oven, he was on his way back, finishing his own naan and feeling almost happy, when he passed a bus. A boy was cleaning the windows—without any energy, Razaq noticed. Just then the driver jumped out of the door. It was the man called Saleem who had brought them down from the mountains. He grabbed Razaq by the arm and hustled him between two buildings, not far from Kazim's restaurant. He turned Razaq to face him.

Razaq bit his lip. "What do you want?"

Saleem half-laughed, his face close to Razaq's. "You are like a mountain wolf, so strong and proud."

Razaq leaned backward. No one had said anything like that to him before, and he didn't like the look in Saleem's eyes. He looked as if he was going to eat him.

"Come now," Saleem's voice wheedled. "It won't take long. I haven't been home for a week. I'll pay you twenty rupees."

Razaq was confused. Twenty rupees sounded good, but what did he have to do? Give him the naan? It had cost fifteen. He'd be five ahead. Razaq slowly held the bread out toward Saleem.

The look in the man's eyes changed. "Bebekoof, you idiot," and he grabbed Razaq and spun him around in one movement and shoved him up against the wall. The naan fell to the ground as Saleem fumbled with his shalwar cord with one hand. Suddenly, Razaq understood.

"No." He twisted to smash out with his fist. "Leave me alone."

He managed to hit Saleem's chin, but Saleem banged his face into the wall and held him there with one arm. Razaq's head spun; he couldn't escape Saleem's grasp, however much he squirmed. He felt the man's body behind him, thrusting to get closer, one hand pushing up his shirt. He tried to kick with his foot, but Saleem had thought of that, too. Razaq was firmly held. Would anyone care if he shouted again?

Suddenly, there was a curse, another voice. "Stop!"

Saleem let Razaq go, and he fell. He scrambled backward out of the way.

"Badmarsh!" It was Kazim and he held a broom. He whacked Saleem over the head with it.

"Stop hitting me, you old devil. I wouldn't hurt him. I just wanted some fun."

"Not with him you can't."

"I didn't know he was yours. Put that broom down!"

Razaq hastily picked up the bread; it was still wrapped in the newspaper. He brushed off the dust and stood near Kazim.

Kazim lowered the broom and Saleem sneered at him. "What do you want with him anyway? You couldn't make your pizzle stand up straight with string."

Kazim's face darkened. "Don't touch him again, sunno? Do you hear?"

"Ji, you stupid bastard." Saleem stomped off to his bus.

Razaq regarded Kazim tentatively. "Shukriya, thank you," he said, but there was no sympathy from Kazim. He smacked Razaq's ear with his open hand.

"What do you think you're doing going down a deserted gali with him?"

"I didn't know."

Kazim stared at Razaq. Then he said, "What are these crumbs on your mouth? You've been eating my naan?"

"Nay, janab, I bought one myself."

Kazim narrowed his eyes. His stillness was more frightening than the beating. For a moment, Razaq thought he was in trouble for eating during Ramadan. Then Kazim said quietly, "You have money? Where did you get it?"

"My father."

"Your father?" Kazim relaxed slightly. "Show me." Razaq took the few rupees from his pocket. Kazim scooped them up. "You don't need this. From now on, I provide for your every need. This will help pay off the exorbitant price I paid for you."

"But—"

"You have too much to say for yourself."

Razaq didn't agree; he hadn't said much at all. His father always told him that none should lord it over another—except the khans, of course, but that was different. They were the ruling barons who owned the land and kept everyone safe, but as far as he knew, they didn't keep slaves. And that's what this felt like.

"Get inside. And next time," Kazim grabbed Razaq's arm, "next time dodge the drivers. They're as randy as dogs and will stick their banana in any hole they see." He gave Razaq a push.

Razaq took the naan into the eating room and laid it on the tables for the customers to eat. The TV was on, and he was beginning to recognize a few actors. The famous Amir Khan was fighting a secret agent in the Kashmiri snow. He noticed a few men stared at him as he watched the screen, until Kazim sent him off to help Aslam.

Razaq had to race for naan again that afternoon. This time, he only took a rupee of his own money. On the way back, he was relieved to see Saleem's bus had gone. The boy who had been cleaning the windows was sitting on the ground eating a cold chapatti.

"You got away from Saleem." The boy said it matter-of-factly. "You haven't been here long?"

Razaq shook his head. The boy was a few years younger than he was, but he had a worn expression, as though he had lived most of his life already. "You work for Saleem? Clean his bus?"

The boy nodded.

"Do you get much money for that?"

The boy shrugged. "Some. It is enough to buy flour and salt to take home."

"You have a family?" Razaq squatted beside him and handed him a piece of his naan.

"My father is crippled now and cannot work. I have sisters." The boy swallowed. "This naan is tasty. My father doesn't ask what I do, just that I bring money home."

"Working on the bus is good?"

The boy looked up and Razaq was shocked to see the bleakness in his eyes. "It is not just the cleaning and getting chai. Saleem protects me from the other men."

Razaq nodded. "Kazim did that for me today."

"Kazim is just protecting his property." The boy paused. "I have to do anything Saleem wants, sometimes it is every day. I thought I would have a rest from it today when he saw you."

Razaq rocked back onto the balls of his feet and blew out a breath. "He does that with you? You let him?"

Defiance sparked in the boy's face. "What else can I do? I have no skills, I cannot even read, and I have to feed my mother and sisters. Better me than them."

"Kazim doesn't do that to me."

The boy's eyes held no pity. "It is just a matter of time."

Razaq thought about it as he washed the dishes throughout the night. His friend Ardil came to mind. Ardil's family were their closest neighbors, but then Ardil was sent to live with one of the khan's friends, all his schooling and upbringing paid for. Now Razaq wondered what Ardil's life had really been like in that stranger's house. Had Ardil seen a look in that man's eyes like Razaq saw in Saleem's, as if he were a goat about to mount a she-goat?

Kazim wouldn't let him go, he knew that now, not when he had paid so much money. To find his uncle, he would have to sneak out when Kazim was asleep in the early hours of the morning. He would have to pick the best day. At least he had his father's purse. He could feed himself until he found his uncle and got another job.

✻

Days dragged by. Razaq's time was so used up he had no energy to think about leaving. He was too tired to do anything early in the morning except collapse onto his blanket. He kept telling himself that he would be used to the hard work soon, and then he would have enough energy to leave, but it seemed as though the more he got used to the work, the more he had to do. He was starting to feel the way Aslam looked: thin and tired. Each morning he'd wake to find Aslam preparing the food. Aslam never did anything quickly, which was the cause for numerous cuffs over the head from Kazim. Razaq received his share, too, if he was too long coming from the tandoor oven.

When he had been there a week, Razaq asked Kazim for his pay. "Can I have what is owed me?"

Kazim was standing at the stove; he whipped around and grabbed Razaq around the neck with one hand. "What's owed you? I'll give you what is owed you." His hand tightened around Razaq's neck. Razaq gagged. "You get no wages until the money I paid for you is made up." He grinned as he released Razaq. "And that will take years."

Razaq coughed and tried again. "The money you paid was commission, not my wages." His voice ended in a squeak.

Kazim pulled back his arm and smacked Razaq across the face. "You ungrateful shaitan. I am feeding you, you have a place to sleep, and you have work to do." For each of those things he hit Razaq over the head. "What more do you want? Most boys have none of this. You should be thanking me for saving you from the streets. Do you know what they do to you out there?" He leaned closer to Razaq. "They gouge your eyes out. Those green eyes would make a rupee or two. Or they take your kidney to sell and forget to sew you up again. Do you want that?" Kazim pulled Razaq's head up. Blood ran from his nose. "What do you say, boy?"

Razaq saw the look in Kazim's eyes, noticed his hand still curled. "Thank you," he mumbled.

"I did not hear you."

"Shukriya, janab." Razaq said it louder and scowled.

Kazim relaxed, stood back a step. "It would be a pity to break that mountain spirit, but by Allah, I will if I have to. And I can, do you understand?"

Razaq managed to get rid of the scowl.

"Go and do your work, and don't get any ideas beyond yourself. You work for me, I look after you. That is all there is to it."

Razaq didn't like the sound of Kazim looking after him. Saleem looked after his boy, too, but what sort of care was that?

※

The next morning when Razaq woke, Aslam's back was toward him. He checked his father's purse. When he opened it, he let out an exclamation of horror.

Aslam didn't even turn. "What is wrong with you?" he said.

"My money. It's gone."

Aslam shrugged. "We are not allowed to keep money."

"You took it," Razaq said, getting into a crouch.

Aslam kept chopping coriander. "He made me." He didn't even sound defensive or sorry.

Razaq stared at his back. Did Aslam have any spirit left? A thought suddenly struck him. "Does Kazim skewer you?"

Aslam shook his head. "Kazim doesn't act like that."

Razaq glanced down at his father's empty purse, then pulled up his head as Aslam carried on. "One of the drivers does."

Razaq pulled Aslam around to face him. "You must tell Kazim. He will stop it—" The words froze on his tongue. Tears were dribbling down Aslam's face.

"Kazim gets paid every time."

"But are you not his nephew?"

"I don't know. He calls me that."

"But that makes Kazim a . . ."

"Ji, a dala. He finds boys for men who want them."

"He stopped Saleem doing it to me."

Aslam's shoulders drooped. "He must have big plans for you then." His gaze dropped to Razaq's purse. "Sorry about your money."

"It was two months' wages at least."

"Not here it wouldn't be. I will never pay off my debt. My father thought he was being paid for an apprenticeship. That is what he thinks I am doing all day—training to be a cook."

"You go home each night. Why do you come back?"

"We need the money—every time I am skewered, Kazim gives me twenty rupees." He shrugged. "If I was not working for Kazim, it would be someone else. At least he looks after me."

"Does he?" Razaq said, then regretted it. What could Aslam do? His family would probably be attacked if he ran away from Kazim. Razaq sighed. At least he didn't have a family who could be held to ransom for his actions. Nor was he going to wait around to be treated like a goat. He gave Aslam a half-smile. "I am going to find Uncle Javaid. He works in a cloth shop in Moti Bazaar."

Razaq thought of all the things he knew about his uncle. He was his father's younger brother. He lived near Raja Bazaar. His wife, Amina, was a girl from the mountains, too, and Uncle Javaid had come home to marry her. Amina was Feeba's cousin. Razaq had been about the age of his sister Seema at the time of the wedding. He remembered the huge degs of curry and rice the barbers had cooked, the music, the men dancing, the guns shooting in the air for joy. His uncle had looked like a prince in a pearled turban as he danced with him. "You're a good dancer, you'll be doing this one day, Razaq," he had said, and grinned, but he'd looked nervous, too. Razaq had gone into the women's tent to see Amina; to his young eyes she had looked like a houri from Paradise. He had always wondered if Feeba would grow up to look like that. He remembered the body they had recovered at the school. There had been too much blood for him to see Feeba's face.

He shook his head clear. Yes, he'd leave today, on his trip to the tandoor oven, money or no money. He'd take the rupees for the naan and be done with it.

Chapter 6

As Javaid came down the mountain, he noticed colored boats with loud tractor engines carrying food supplies docking at the village. A few Western people from the boats brought the supplies to shore. Tents were lined up near the river, and he strolled down there, but without calling outside the tent flaps, he couldn't tell if anyone he knew was inside. He carried on past the tents until he came to the end of the rows. A woman was tending a fire with a saucepan bubbling above it, no doubt a meal for when the fast ended. The woman saw him and quickly covered her face with her shawl. She looked familiar, like one of Amina's aunties.

"Auntie ji?" he said.

She glanced up at him. "Nadeem?"

"No, I am his brother. Have you seen him?"

She shook her head slightly.

"Have you had much loss?" he asked gently.

"All my family, except my son."

"I am very sorry to hear that."

She brightened. "But my son has gone to the city to get a job. He will return with money to build me a house."

Javaid stared at her in pity. If she was the aunt he thought she was, she had suffered greatly. She wasn't making sense at all. How could one young man make enough money to build a house? He excused himself and walked toward some tents where children were playing soccer. He quickened his steps. There was a colorful sign saying: *You have the right to play.* He frowned—it sounded like a Western outfit.

"Yes?" A young white woman was inside the tent with a group of girls. Like a flock of birds taking flight, the girls covered their heads with one sweep of their hands. The woman was startling to look at, and he averted his eyes.

"I am sorry to intrude, but I am looking for my family," he said in English.

The woman asked an older girl to take the class, then she said to Javaid, "Come with me." She took him to another tent where a man sat at a desk.

"I am looking for Nadeem Khan's family," Javaid said to him.

The man opened a book that looked like a ledger. "We are trying to keep track of who survived," he said, crinkling his forehead. He checked on many pages while Javaid waited, then finally shook his head.

Javaid wished the man would look again. "They had children: a boy, Razaq, about fourteen, and two younger girls, Seema and Layla?"

"Did you say Razaq?" the woman said. Her English was fast and difficult to understand. "A boy named Razaq came here."

"Razaq Nadeem Khan?" Javaid hardly dared hope.

She thought a moment. "I don't know, he didn't say. He was helping for a day or two, but he hasn't returned."

Javaid glanced at the book. "Would you not have written it down?"

The man looked up. "I only started the records yesterday."

Javaid addressed the woman again. "What did this Razaq look like?"

The woman smiled. She was looking into his face openly as only Western women did. Javaid had to deal with such women in the shop sometimes; they even spoke to him if their husbands were with them, but he knew they didn't mean any harm. It was just the way they were raised.

"He had the most unusual green eyes," the woman said. "Good looking, helpful, and respectful."

Javaid was so aghast he forgot his manners and stared at her. Green eyes? Didn't he himself have light-colored eyes? And respectful? She had just described practically every boy in the mountains. Only politeness stopped him from cursing. How would he find Razaq? With no maulvi, he couldn't get a message out.

He turned to the man. "Who is giving the azan, the call to prayer?"

"Wazir Ahmad, the maulvi's son. He is living behind the mosque."

Javaid inclined his head to the young woman without looking at her directly this time and retreated to the village. He bought a chicken kebab and ate it with a chapatti by the side of the road. He stripped the chunks of meat from the bamboo skewer and slowly ate each piece wrapped in strips of the bread. The food in Kala Dhaka was the best he had ever eaten. Food in the city could never match it for freshness and taste.

He wiped his hands and hurried on toward the mosque. "Janab!" he called at the door.

"Ji?" A man with a long black beard emerged from a tent to the side.

"Why do you not sleep in the mosque, janab?" Javaid asked.

"We are having many aftershocks. All the people are frightened of buildings collapsing."

"I am searching for Nadeem Khan. He is my brother."

The man frowned in thought. "I do not think I know him."

"He lives in the mountains," Javaid said.

Wazir Ahmad sighed. "We found some survivors and brought them down. But there were many wounded we could not help."

"Were there a boy and two girls?"

"There were many boys and girls." He put a hand on Javaid's shoulder. "Do not worry, bhai, I will ask when I give the call to prayer."

He sounded weary and Javaid wondered how many people he had told not to worry in the past week.

"Please be sure to say all the names: Nadeem Khan, Mrs. Nadeem, Razaq, Seema, Layla."

"Zarur, certainly."

❋

Javaid waited for the evening prayer near a tent that was set up as a shop. He would have to give thought to where he would sleep tonight. His eyes began to close: the bus trip had taken its toll, plus that walk up to Nadeem's holding. He wrapped himself in his shawl and lay on the ground near the mosque. He was woken in the late afternoon by the azan. Wazir Ahmad was wielding a megaphone in front of the mosque. It looked as though he was taking no chances on the minaret. At the end of the prayers, he mentioned the names of Javaid's family and some others as well. Javaid did his namaz, hoping God would see his devotion and help him.

When he finished his prayers, he saw two boys, almost men, with Wazir Ahmad. They were mountain boys with AK-47s slung over their shoulders as proudly as city boys wore a gold watch on their wrist. When Wazir Ahmad saw Javaid walking toward them, he said, "Janab, these boys may be able to help you. They are Abdul and Hussain."

The shorter one named Hussain spoke. "We know a boy named Razaq, but we do not know if he is your relative."

"We helped him bury his father," said the other boy, Abdul.

Javaid's heart plummeted. Still, it may not be Nadeem. "Where is he now?"

"We haven't seen him recently."

"Not since we helped him fight off thieves from his mother's tent a few nights ago," Hussain added.

Javaid couldn't contain his anxiety. "His mother is here? Mrs. Nadeem?"

"He called her Mrs. Daud," Hussain said.

Javaid couldn't help himself. He burst out, "Could you please take me to her?"

"Zarur, certainly," Hussain said.

Javaid followed them to the lines of tents by the river. When they made their way to the very same tent he had already visited, he had conflicting feelings. Since this wasn't Nadeem's wife, perhaps Nadeem was still alive. But the alternative was worrying: where was his nephew? He thought of the grave. How tall would Razaq be now?

The woman was inside the tent. "Mrs. Daud?" Hussain called. "I am a friend of your son's."

Mrs. Daud emerged from the tent, a shawl around her head and face. "Have you word of him?"

"No, but this man is looking for his relatives."

Mrs. Daud looked up at Javaid, but there was no recognition in her eyes that he had been there before. "My son has gone to the city to find work."

"How did he do that?" Hussain asked.

"A man took him. And he gave me money," she said proudly.

"What do you mean?" Abdul's voice was tight.

"The man said he would give him a job."

"But Razaq—"

Javaid cut in. "Do you have a signed paper? What was the man's name?"

Mrs. Daud shut her eyes. "I think it was Ikram."

"And a family name?" Javaid asked, trying to keep his voice level.

She shifted her head to one side. "He did not say."

Javaid suspected there was no signed paper either.

Hussain looked at her in disbelief. "You let a man you do not know take Razaq away—how much money did he give you?"

"Three hundred rupees," she said happily.

"But that is stupid—how could you do that to your son—"

Javaid laid a hand on Hussain's shoulder. When the boy glanced up, Javaid shook his head slightly. They moved away.

"She has suffered much trauma," he said. "She would not have known what she was doing."

"I am sorry about your nephew," Abdul said.

"Thank you for your concern," Javaid said, "but your friend Razaq is not my nephew."

Abdul frowned at him. "How can you know this for certain?"

"It is simple. Mrs. Daud is not my nephew's mother. She is the aunt of my wife."

❋

Javaid stayed on in the village; he felt closer to Nadeem there. One night, there was a bigger aftershock than usual. He woke, ready to run, but it subsided. He lay down again, wrapped in his shawl under a makeshift shelter created from a sheet. Not for the first time he felt the old stirrings of doubt. Maybe he shouldn't have gone to the city. He remembered one of the worst shouting matches with Nadeem. Was he right that Javaid shirked his responsibility, that he wasn't a true mountain man? If he had been here, could he have helped Nadeem and the family, or would he have died like so many others? He had seen the village burial ground, but the maulvi did not have his brother listed. Maybe Nadeem had taken his family elsewhere for aid.

That day he ate at different stalls in the bazaar, asking about Nadeem, but no one had news. He had tried talking again to Mrs. Daud in case she remembered anything new. Something would have to be done about her. She was Amina's aunt, and where was her brother? Why hadn't he come to take her home to live with him?

Hussain and Abdul came to see him at the mosque that afternoon. "We are worried about Razaq," Hussain said.

"And I am not convinced he isn't your nephew," Abdul added. "He protected Mrs. Daud as we would any female relative, but he never referred to her as his mother. He told us he had lost all his family."

"We think we should show you the grave we helped him dig," Hussain said.

"To put our minds at rest." Abdul sounded like an echo.

Javaid stood and shifted his feet. "I have seen the burial grounds here," he said. "Wazir Ahmad has no record of my brother."

"The grave is in the mountains," Hussain said, watching Javaid carefully.

Javaid stiffened. What good would all this do? Maybe he should just go home today.

"Please," Abdul said. "It is making our hearts heavy."

Javaid sighed. "Okay. Show me."

The boys took him up the same path he had climbed days before. With each step the sense of foreboding in his heart grew, but he tried to keep it at bay. Hundreds of families used this path. Then the boys led him to Nadeem's holding. Without knowing how he got there, Javaid found himself staring at the grave with rocks on it.

Hussain spoke quietly. "This is Razaq's father. A tree had fallen on him. No one else survived." Hussain gestured toward the pile of rubble that had once been a shale and mud house.

For the second time that week, Javaid sank to his knees.

The boys retreated to wait while Javaid stretched himself over the grave.

"Bhai jan, I am so sorry." The tears flowed but he spoke through them, hoping his brother could hear. "I am sorry, you were right—I should have been here. But I will make amends. Do not worry, brother. God help me, I will find Razaq."

Chapter 7

Razaq woke at noon. He barely had his eyes open before Kazim was throwing orders at him: fill buckets with water, help peel vegetables. "We are run off our feet today," Kazim said. "Everyone is on their way to the cricket at Lahore. You," he pointed at Razaq, "you have to help Aslam as well."

Razaq picked up a vegetable knife, but Kazim smacked him over the head. "No, get thirty naan first." He handed Razaq the money.

Razaq slapped his pakol on his head and pulled on his father's sandals as Kazim flapped back to the eating room. They almost fit him now. Aslam watched him. Razaq could tell he was wondering why he was wearing shoes.

He winked at Aslam. "If I get rich and famous, like Amir Khan, I will come back and help you." He chuckled as Aslam's mouth dropped open. It was the way he thought he would always remember Aslam.

Outside, the bus adda was busier than usual. Buses revved their engines; men shouted; boys called their wares of shoelaces, Sprite, and ices. He saw Saleem's boy carrying curry and chapatti to the bus, for Saleem no doubt. Razaq ducked his head and made off toward the tandoor oven. He had thirty rupees in his pocket; he bought two naan, one for now and one for later.

"Only two?" the boy said. "I thought you would want many with the crowd today."

Razaq realized too late it had been a mistake to buy food there. He shrugged as if he had all the time in the world. "The other boy is getting them today." And he scooted off.

Razaq didn't dare stop to ask anyone the way until he couldn't see the tandoor shop. When he finally asked where Raja Bazaar was, a man said it was a long distance.

"Can I walk?" Razaq asked.

The man shook his head. "Bus is the quickest and cheapest way."

Razaq looked at him in dismay. He couldn't go back to the bus adda now. What if Kazim saw him before the bus left? Besides, many people who worked there might know he was Kazim's boy and give him away. He stood by the side of the road, thinking what to do, when a rickshaw pulled up beside him. Razaq had never ridden in one. It shook and spat out black fumes.

"Get in," the driver said. "Where do you want to go?"

"Raja Bazaar, janab."

Razaq climbed in behind the driver and watched the streets fly past. Every now and then he caught the driver studying him in the mirror, but Razaq couldn't take his eyes from the streets for long. The shops were so much bigger than anything he'd seen in the village on the Indus. Yes, there were buffaloes on the street, and carts pulled by horses, but also many cars, trucks, and motorbikes, and all tooting at once. There was even a train going over a bridge above him. He had heard of trains. It was noisy, too, but the put-put of the rickshaw gaining speed soon drowned it out.

When they pulled to a stop among busy shops with stalls spilling onto the pavement, the driver said, "That will be twenty rupees."

"So much?" Razaq stared at the man in horror.

The man grunted. "I didn't think you would have any money. You are not from Rawalpindi, are you?"

"How did you know?"

The driver looked at Razaq's eyes, his brown hair and mountain lambswool hat and said, "You did not check the price before you got in. I could have asked you for any amount. Have you not been in a rickshaw before?"

Razaq shook his head.

"It is free for you," the man said, then added, "Not everyone will look after you, so think before you act when someone tells you to get in his rickshaw. Where are you going?"

"To find my uncle. He lives in a mohalla near Raja Bazaar."

"This is Raja Bazaar—may Allah go with you."

"Shukriya." Razaq dipped his head and climbed out so quickly he stumbled over an open drain. A bicycle bell scolded him, and a beggar asked for money. Razaq made a mental note not to travel in a rickshaw again; even the beggars thought he was richer than them.

A food wallah shouted his wares in Razaq's face as he pushed his cart: "Piazay! Onions! Five rupees."

Nearby, two men in white shalwar qameezes broke into a fight. "You cheated me," the older one cried. "Give me the proper change."

Razaq stared, fascinated, as an old man came out of the shop and slapped the younger man over the head. The younger man reached into his pocket and pulled out some money. The aggrieved man took it and walked on toward Razaq.

Razaq thought someone who knew he'd been given the wrong change would know many things, like where Uncle Javaid lived. He stepped forward as the man came closer. "Janab, excuse me?"

The man slowed, but frowned. "I have nothing to give you," he said.

What did he see, Razaq wondered: a boy in need of help or a street beggar? The man made to walk on, but Razaq said, "I just need to know where my uncle lives, Javaid Khan. He lives near here, behind Raja Bazaar."

The man smirked. "You crazy kid, what God-forsaken place have you crawled out from? You know how many people live here? Thousands. You need an address—what street, what gali?"

Razaq had a sinking feeling in his stomach, but he tried again. "He works in a cloth shop in Moti Bazaar."

The man laughed. "How many cloth shops are there in Moti Bazaar? How many hairs on a dog?" Then he looked at Razaq as if seeing him for the first time. He sighed. "Go to Moti Bazaar and ask there."

"Where is it?"

The man gestured toward the south. "Go to Fawara Chowk, then turn east onto Iqbal Road."

"Shukriya." Razaq laid his hand over his heart as his father did at such times and walked on. He took a peek back at the man and saw him talking to another man who was smoking outside a shop. Both were shaking their heads.

People in the mountains were suspicious of new people coming into the tribal areas. Razaq was surprised to find city people were the same. He hoped he didn't do anything to annoy someone. What if there were different rules here? Once, an Angrez had ridden a bicycle into Kala Dhaka. He didn't wear proper clothes and much of his white skin showed. He stopped to speak to a woman and the woman's husband shot him. He was obviously a dala; he'd be raping her next or taking her away. You couldn't trust a man who spoke to a woman who wasn't his relative.

Razaq reached the chowk. Six roads met at the intersection, and it teemed with cars, buses, bicycles, and rickshaws, all converging like a knot in six lengths of string. And just like a knot they found it difficult to unravel. The tooting of horns and shouting from car windows was deafening. There was even a buffalo in the middle of the chowk. It plodded on without concern as the drivers swerved around it. Razaq jumped out into the traffic. A car blared its horn; another braked with a squeal. He raced in front of a bus and reached the buffalo. She had a frayed rope hanging from her neck.

"A jao, come," he murmured, "you need the side of the road." The buffalo's brown eyes met his, and he was shocked at how tired and listless she looked. Peepu's eyes always glistened with humor. "Come," he coaxed, pushing away the image of the ram lifeless on the ground. He finally navigated the lanes of traffic, ignoring the cursing from drivers, and got the buffalo to the mud footpath where there were blades of grass she could nibble.

A man in khaki trousers like a foreigner's spoke to him. "And what do you think you are doing, boy?"

Razaq's heart thundered in his chest. He must have broken a rule.

"We are trying to keep buffaloes out of the traffic in the city," the man said.

Razaq noticed the badge on the man's shirt, his hat, his stick to hit criminals with. He was either army or police. "That is what I was doing, janab. I was rescuing her."

"So she is yours?"

Razaq shook his head.

"You were stealing her then." The man's hand rested on the baton in his belt.

"No, but I know about animals—they like fields best."

The man smirked. "I am sure they do. Get going then."

"The buffalo—"

"Its owner will find it."

Razaq thought he shouldn't argue anymore, but the buffalo wrung his heart. His goats and sheep at home had been fat and happy. This buffalo's skin barely stretched across her ribs and haunches. He knew how to make her better, too—if only he could take her out of the city, she would find enough food to eat. But one more look at the man's face, stiff and stern, made him walk away.

He asked a man selling shoelaces which of the roads was Iqbal Road.

"I can clean your shoes," the man answered.

"No, thank you," Razaq said. Did he look like someone who could waste his money on shoeshining?

"Then I cannot tell you which one is the road."

Razaq moved on. Why would someone want money to give a simple direction? He asked at a shop, but got shooed away as if he were a beggar.

Finally, a boy about his age told him he knew, but his eyes were canny. "Come with me," he said, "and I'll show you."

"I do not have money to give you," Razaq said as a precaution.

The boy looked at Razaq's feet. "Nice sandals."

Razaq's eyes flashed. "They are my dead father's."

"Teik hai, okay, don't burst into flames. That one is Iqbal Road." The boy indicated the busiest road. "I will take you there."

Razaq followed the boy across two roads, jumping between vehicles. Cars screeched, horns tooted and yet, surprisingly, this time no one seemed angry.

"I do this all the time," the boy said when they reached the side of Iqbal Road. "Where do you want to go?"

Razaq hesitated, then thought it couldn't hurt to say. "Moti Bazaar."

"Then you have to cross Iqbal Road as well—the bazaar is over there."

Razaq sighed. He had done it by himself when he rescued the buffalo; he could do it again. "Shukriya," he said.

"You're not from here, are you?"

Razaq glanced at the boy in surprise.

"Be careful. I know you are alone—you have that look. Others will see it, too, so watch your eyes. My name is Zakim. I live here on the street."

"Here?"

Zakim made a curious gesture with his eyebrows and nose. "I have a place. If you need help, ask for me."

Razaq stared at him. How could Zakim help him—he only looked about fourteen, like himself. "I am looking for my uncle, Javaid Khan," he said, to show he didn't need help.

"Accha, good. God go with you then."

Razaq smiled his thanks and plunged into Iqbal Road. He had learned something from Zakim: you just ran across without looking, like swinging in a basket across a mountain stream, and God let the traffic stop for you. When he reached the other side, he stood there panting, but Zakim was nowhere to be seen. He grinned. It had been exhilarating with Zakim. In that moment, he felt hope uncurl in his belly. He would find Uncle Javaid. He just had to ask in all the shops in Moti Bazaar even if it took all day.

He found an iron archway. There were words on top. He sounded them out to himself. There was a meem first: M-O-T-I. Yes, he was where he was meant to be. He sauntered down the gali. Shops lined the tiny street and there was a covering overhead. It was like walking down a tunnel of trees in the forest.

He asked for Javaid Khan at the first cloth shop. The man there waved him away; he was too busy even to open his mouth. At the tenth shop, the man came out to the gali with him. "Look," he said and pointed up the gali. "Can you see the end of this bazaar?"

Razaq gave a slight shake of his head.

"And not only does it stretch so far you cannot see its end, there are many side streets. It will be Eid before you can visit each one. You need the name of the shop or the name of the owner. Does your uncle own it?"

"I do not know." Razaq's voice was quiet.

The man pursed his mouth. "You will just be chasing your tail." He looked Razaq up and down. "From up north, are you? From the earthquake?"

"Ji, janab."

"If you get a problem, you can come back here and sleep outside my shop until you find him."

Razaq opened his mouth to thank him, but the man went on. "You can be my chowkidar. In return I will give you an evening meal."

Razaq wasn't sure what sort of chowkidar he would be. What if thieves came and beat him while he was protecting the shop? But he had saved Mrs. Daud's tent, though that was mainly due to Abdul and Hussain turning up. Still, a job was a job.

"Thank you, janab," he said.

"What is your name, beta?"

"Razaq."

"You are a khan, I suppose—all you mountain people are."

Razaq didn't answer. It wasn't true they were all khans, even though his father's family bore the name. The man didn't give his name in return, and Razaq didn't feel he could ask. It wouldn't be polite. He checked the name of the shop, Deen's Cloth, before he continued along the gali, asking for his uncle.

There were women everywhere; he'd never seen so many at once except at a wedding. Some didn't even wear a burqa, and a few girls his age wore tight blue trousers like men and a scarf slung around their necks instead of over their hair. He stared so long at one woman as she walked toward him with her friends that she pinched his face when she reached him. It was something his mother playfully did when she was happy with him.

The woman was very tall with much makeup on her face, and a deep voice. "So what's a pretty mountain boy like you doing in the city?"

How did she know he was from the mountains? It was as though there was a big sign above his head.

"You need to buy a different hat." She touched his lambswool pakol. "City boys don't wear these." As she moved away, she blew between her fingers at him and winked. Razaq was stunned. He had never known a woman to speak to a boy his age before. Though since he was short and didn't have a mustache yet, she may have thought he was younger.

He had long stopped counting the shops when he came to one with a TV showing the cricket match in Lahore. Some men were watching the TV while their women fingered the silk cloths. Razaq asked the youngest shop worker if a Javaid Khan worked there. A guarded look came over the young man's face. Razaq had seen that look before—it meant the man thought he was going to ask for money or food. He steeled himself for what would come next.

"Get lost," the young man said. "We've given enough to kids like you today."

It was late and Razaq's stomach rumbled. He made his way back through the warren of shops until he found Deen's. The man was already eating when Razaq greeted him.

"Find your uncle, beta?"

Razaq gave a tired shake of his head. The man didn't look sympathetic, but he pushed over a chapatti and moved his bowl of curry closer to Razaq.

"Eat up," he said. "Chowkidaring is hard work." He chuckled, but Razaq couldn't see what was funny.

When the food was gone, the man pulled down the shutters of the shop and laid a mat on the footpath in front. Razaq knew he wouldn't be a good chowkidar for at least a few hours. When he lay down, he couldn't keep his eyes open.

He dreamed of his mother. She looked right into his eyes, and he could see the green ringing her black pupils. He had inherited her eyes; his father's were gray like his sisters'. "Beta, this is not a good job for you," his mother said. "Wake up. You need to cut the grass for the goats. If your father catches you sleeping, he will beat you. In the village, I am called the mother of Abdur-Razaq, so make me proud of that name, beta. Wake up now or the wolves will find you."

"Wake up."

"What?" Razaq opened one eye and sat up suddenly. Someone was shaking him. "Zakim? What are you doing here?"

There were pale lights shining on the walls, sweepers were cleaning the gali, and most of the customers had gone.

Zakim glanced up the bazaar. "We have to get out of here." He tried to pull Razaq up.

"I am a chowkidar—I cannot leave."

"Fool. If you've been asked to work, it is a lie. Men come here to find lone boys lying outside shops. They will make you a slave. Do you want that?"

Thoughts of Kazim crowded Razaq's mind, and he jumped to his feet. "Of course not."

There was the sound of footsteps. A group of men entered the gali from the road.

"They're coming. Chello, I'll show you a way out."

Chapter 8

Zakim led Razaq down a side gali Razaq hadn't seen that afternoon. The men were close behind. Razaq had the impression of sticks, rough voices, and curses.

"This way," Zakim shouted. He pushed himself into what looked like a round drainpipe. Razaq hesitated.

"Jaldi ao, quickly! They'll see you."

A noise from the gali made Razaq plunge in after him. The drain stank. His mother would have made him wash in the river if he came home stinking like this. He held his breath—the pipe couldn't last forever. When they finally emerged, they were outside. A breeze ruffled the hair sticking out from under Razaq's hat and the moon was shining. He could tell Zakim was grinning at him.

"How did you find me?"

Zakim laughed. "I thought I'd better keep an eye on you—a babe among wolves."

Razaq stiffened. That was what his mother had said in the dream. Zakim touched Razaq's cheek lightly, then pinched it harder than the lady in the bazaar had.

"Hey!"

"Do not worry, I like you. They say brides are as beautiful and pale as the moon, but I bet they don't match mountain boys like you. That is what I will call you—Chandi, after the moon. It's why I looked for you, in case someone else thought the same. Besides, I'm often patrolling some bazaar or other at night. I never know what I'll find. Once I found a wallet with a wad of rupees. It kept us fed for a month."

"Us?"

Zakim regarded him a moment. "I am not alone. You can join us if you like." He laughed at Razaq's confused expression. "In the morning you will see, Chandi. Follow me, I'll show you where you can sleep."

Razaq didn't wake until mid-morning. When he opened his eyes, he was shut inside a huge cardboard box. He felt a rush of panic and then he remembered Zakim. Three small children sat cross-legged watching him. He sat up, blinking sleep away. "Where am I?"

"This is the Rag Mahal," the tallest girl said. She had lost a tooth like his youngest sister, Layla, and when she spoke, she reminded Razaq so strongly of her he winced.

"A palace?" he murmured.

The boy stood up. Razaq tried not to stare at him for he was disfigured: he had no nose, only holes in his face, and his arms were too short and so were his legs.

"My name is Raj," he said. "This is Hira, she is the youngest, and this is Moti." His voice was strange: muffled and lisping, as if part of his mouth was missing inside. "Moti is named after the Moti Bazaar because Zakim found her alone there when she was little."

"But it means pearl," Moti added with pride.

Razaq studied the gap in her teeth. How long had Zakim been living like this? Six years?

"Why do you have green eyes?" Raj asked. "Are you magic? A genie?" He sounded hopeful.

"I do not think so," Razaq said. He searched the solemn faces in front of him. "Did Zakim find you all?"

"Of course," Moti said. "Didn't he find you?"

"He gives us all a name," Raj said. "And now we have to show you what to do. We work here."

Razaq crawled out of the shelter to see what the boy meant. Before him was a mountain of garbage. He had never seen so much rubbish. At home, his mother had made use of most things, and what the goats wouldn't eat, he had buried.

Moti followed close behind him. "One day we will be rich."

"Like princes," Raj added.

Hira took his hand. She looked about four years old. "You do look like the moon," she said.

Razaq felt his face grow hot. Chandi was going to be an embarrassing nickname. He blew out a breath. "What do you do all day?" he asked.

Moti took his other hand. "We find good rubbish and Zakim sells it. Sprite bottles are the best. But sometimes we just have to pick up paper and rags. Zakim says someone uses them again." She scrunched up her face.

"Zakim picks up metal scrap," Raj said.

"Is it dangerous?" Razaq was thinking of accidents with broken glass or the little ones falling off the dump and wasn't ready for Raj's answer.

"We just have to watch out for the slavers."

Razaq looked quickly at him. "The what?"

"The men who want to take us away from Zakim," Moti said. "They will tell us they have a nice place for us to sleep, but really they want us to be slaves and beg for them. Here we are free. So we watch out for each other. If you see any men, run away." Razaq let her pull him forward. "Just find nice things to sell," she went on. "Then we can have tasty khana tonight. Usually we just have chapatti and chai, and boiled potatoes if Zakim is lucky."

"Ji," said Hira, "but last night we ate shami kebabs. The meat in them was tasty."

"They were cold and moldy," Raj reminded her.

Hira pouted. "I still liked them."

Moti found Razaq a huge plastic bag, and he soon learned what was salable: soft-drink bottles and jars, rags for car shops. If he brought anything back that couldn't be sold, Moti looked at him mournfully. He couldn't stand it. He imagined how he'd feel if he had to find things to sell so Seema and Layla could eat that night and worked so hard he didn't notice Zakim come up behind him.

"You've taken to the scrap yard, I see."

Razaq spun around. Zakim had a canvas bag over his shoulder and a jacket in his hand. It was green and looked like it belonged to a cricketer.

"This is for you," he said. "You were shivering in your sleep last night. I found it in Landar Bazaar."

Razaq didn't immediately take it so Zakim held it out. "You can pay me later."

"Shukriya."

Zakim watched him trying it on, then said, "You must have left quickly from where you were not to take a coat."

Razaq nodded, not sure how to explain Kazim in the freedom of the morning sun. He took the jacket off and tied it around his waist. Zakim wasn't smiling today, he noticed. "Is anything the matter?"

Zakim glanced at the children picking up garbage. Moti's voice carried up the dump, telling them what to do. "I want to keep them safe," he said.

Razaq was silent with respect.

"But there is someone who doesn't want that."

"Who?"

"The bear."

Razaq stared at him, crinkling his eyes.

"Nasir Ali," Zakim explained. "He works the other side of the dump. He wants my section, too."

"He will not treat the children well?"

"No."

"Then he must be stopped."

Zakim grunted. "And you have an idea how to do that, mountain boy?"

Razaq thought of his and his father's rifles buried under the destroyed house. "Do you have a gun?"

Zakim gaped at him. "A gun?"

"It is how we protected our family and herds from wild animals. Everyone in the mountains had one. It was very effective."

Zakim glanced at the cardboard shelter and back to Razaq. "The bear has a knife."

"You do not?"

"It is my knife he has."

"So you have fought before." It was a statement not a question. "How much is a knife?"

"I know where to get a used one for twenty-five rupees."

Razaq thought a moment. Did Zakim know how much money he had? He glanced at Moti and Raj, who were cajoling Hira to keep picking up papers, then lifted his chin just as his father did when he had made a decision. He pulled the money out of his pocket.

When he looked up, Zakim was grinning. "I knew I hadn't picked you up for nothing, Chandi."

When Zakim returned that evening, he had two knives and dinner in a square plastic box.

"How—" Razaq began.

"Don't ask, Chandi." Zakim passed him a knife.

The little children sat in an eager circle around the box of curry, and Zakim handed out chapattis. Razaq suspected his money had paid for the food so how did Zakim get the knives? Zakim saw him watching him and made that curious gesture with his eyebrows and nose. Razaq grinned. He guessed he was never going to find out. He joined in with the others, scooping curry up with pieces of chapatti.

"Just like my mother used to make," Zakim said with a sigh.

"I say it is not," Raj said.

Zakim looked at the boy with mock sadness. "You need to use your imagination more, Raj."

The cardboard shelter had been made with the same care that Razaq's father had taken when building their house. Part of it was a box that some sort of machine had been sold in, which Zakim had tied together with another box. Over the top were sheets of plastic, then more scraps of cardboard held down with wire.

"Welcome to our palace," he said and ushered Razaq inside, where he lit a candle.

Moti put the other two and herself to sleep on a cardboard mat at the back of the box. Zakim laid a thin blanket over them then came to sit with Razaq near the opening. He pulled a tube from a small bag.

"What is that?" Razaq asked.

Zakim squeezed something out of the tube onto a piece of dirty cloth and handed it to Razaq. "You sniff it."

"Why?"

"It makes you feel better. Helps you forget you haven't eaten or are only a prince of a small part of a rubbish dump. It can even make you feel warm—no need for blankets. Magic." He grinned.

Razaq frowned. "It is like hashish?"

"Hash is too expensive."

"In the mountains, men who smoke too much hash cannot fight."

Zakim lowered the cloth. "What is it you are meaning?"

Razaq ignored the threat in Zakim's voice. "What if the bear comes tonight? He would finish you off."

Zakim brought the cloth to his nose. "This will make me forget about him."

"Then you will not realize when he kills you. I would rather know when I am being killed." He lowered his voice. "Maybe the two of us can overpower him."

Zakim shook his head. "He is a bear."

"Bears still have blood like we do, and it pours out like ours. Even a bear feels pain when a ring is put in its nose."

Razaq watched Zakim put the cloth away. A gun or a knife was no protection against an earthquake, but the bear surely couldn't be as strong as the earth in a rage.

Chapter 9

When Javaid arrived home from the tribal areas, Sakina jumped into his arms as soon as he entered the courtyard. "Abu, why were you away so long? I missed you."

"I missed you too, beti."

Javaid held her close against him. How good it was to smell her freshly washed hair and feel her vibrancy. Amina laid her hand on his back, and he dropped his head to her shoulder and let out a sob.

"It was bad?" she whispered.

He lifted his head and gave them both a watery smile. "I have brought someone to stay with us." His voice broke, but he carried on. "She is the only relative I could find alive."

Amina's eyes filled and then she saw her aunt behind him. "Auntie Latifa?" She enveloped her aunt in a hug, then looked back at Javaid, a question on her face.

"There was no one else," he said. "Her brother hadn't come. Perhaps he couldn't—he lives in Azad Kashmir. They were hit worse than Kala Dhaka. And it's getting cold up there."

"My uncle? Their sons? Feeba?"

Javaid shook his head. "All of the children were in the madrasah . . ." He choked back another sob and glanced at Latifa, but she seemed unperturbed.

Sakina stared intently at his face. She put a finger to his eye. "Abu is sad."

He was loathe to put her down, so he kept her in one arm as he brought in his bag and Latifa's few things.

Latifa was talking to Amina inside the house. "My son will send me money soon, so do not worry. It is very kind of you to have me."

Amina frowned at Javaid. He put Sakina near Latifa to say salaam and took Amina into the second room.

"She speaks of Razaq," he told her. "He is still alive, and she thinks he is her son. It is the grief. She cannot bear the burden of it so I humor her. But I have to find Razaq and bring him here."

He searched her face, and she nodded.

"We will have a houseful," she said.

"It is our way." He smiled. "The best way to live. When Razaq gets married, we can build another room."

"Where is he?"

Javaid sank onto the charpoy. "Auntie Latifa says a man took him for a job here in Rawalpindi."

"But he could have been anyone." Amina glanced out at her aunt. "No one gives a job for nothing."

"She didn't know what she was doing. But I fear for Razaq." Javaid glanced at Amina before he said the next sentence. "The man may have been a slaver."

Amina laid a hand on Javaid's. "Then Razaq could be anywhere by now. How will you find him?"

Javaid closed his eyes a moment. When he opened them he said quietly, "I don't know."

�֍

During his lunch break the first day back at Fazal Clothing Emporium, Javaid sat at the computer and keyed in the words "slave trade." He was appalled at what he found. Hundreds of thousands of children were sold each year, and it was even happening in Pakistan. Many were sold into domestic positions or carpet or brick factories. Some were even forced into prostitution. The given cause for this one? Segregation of the sexes. He swore under his breath. This was a Muslim country. Any decent man wouldn't hurt a child surely?

He searched government sites. Trafficking was illegal, Programs were in place to help, even a government bureau to help eradicate child beggary and to rescue trafficked children. There were nigeban, government-run shelters, for kidnapped or lost boys. He would check those, and the bus terminals heading north. Nongovernment organizations were also set up to rehabilitate children. He took down the details in a small notebook and popped it in his qameez pocket.

Winter would set in soon. He hoped Razaq was still in the city and hadn't been sent to the Gulf States, though he was too old to be a camel jockey. Javaid had read how some boys were sent there and even to Europe. He would have to search quickly for he had no finance for overseas travel.

First stop: the bus adda where the bus most likely to have brought Razaq down from Kala Dhaka would have terminated. Was it too obvious? Would he have been taken elsewhere? The information Javaid had read showed the bus terminals were rife with crime. He logged off. He would start searching the biggest bus adda that night.

The busiest and most northern bus adda in Rawalpindi was like an ants' nest when Javaid arrived. It was the same bus station from where he had traveled north after the earthquake. Twelve thousand buses passed through the dusty grounds in twenty-four hours. He climbed out of the rickshaw he had hired, paid the man, and stared around him. How did he think he could do this? There were hundreds of kacha stalls, teashops, boys walking around selling drinks or washing buses even at this time of night. He had never noticed before how many young boys were employed here. It had all just been part of the scenery. But that was before he had to find Razaq.

He started with the boys standing around selling shoelaces. "Do you know a boy named Razaq?" he asked one. He got only a blank stare; the boy looked drugged.

An older boy walked up to him. "Malish, massage," he said in Javaid's face, rattling his oil bottles in a tiny steel crate.

Javaid shook his head.

"I do good malish, janab."

Javaid tried to ignore him.

"What you want?" The boy lifted his chin. "I do whatever you want."

Javaid was appalled. How old was this boy? Fifteen at the most.

The boy smiled at him and tilted his head from side to side. "Ji, janab. Come with me. You will be happy."

"No," Javaid managed to say. "I am busy looking for someone."

"Who you looking for? I can help. Anything I can do."

Javaid realized he wasn't going to get rid of this boy easily. He looked Afghan. Was this what Razaq would be like if he didn't find him soon?

"A boy," Javaid said. "A boy with green eyes."

The boy laughed. "You want a boy? I am a boy. You want green eyes. I can find the contact lens, na?"

"No, not any boy." Javaid closed his eyes a moment. "I am looking for my nephew."

It was the way he said it; it made the boy put a hand in front of his chest in concern. "Teik hai, janab, I understand. Please, ask the bus boys, they see everything."

"Thank you," Javaid said and handed the boy ten rupees.

The boy didn't take it. "Nay, janab. I wish someone had looked for me when I was young." Then he grinned again. "But now it is too late, and malish business is very good. Someone will give me five hundred rupees tonight. Keep it for the bus boys."

Javaid didn't have much success with the bus boys. Some were so tired they simply ignored him. Others looked at him in fear as if he was propositioning them. As more time went by, the sadder and sicker he felt. Surely something could be done for these children.

He stood still, catching his bearings. Perhaps he should try the buses that only traveled north. Didn't the buses always park in the same place? He was directed to two different stands before he found the place where he'd caught the bus to Oghi. He approached a boy with a bucket and cloth washing the windscreen of a bus with "Oghi" painted above it. "Have you seen a boy named Razaq? A mountain boy with green eyes."

The young boy took no notice until Javaid mentioned green eyes. Then he put his cloth in the bucket and stared at

Javaid. "I met a boy with green eyes," he finally said. "I had never seen such a one as him. He looked like a pari, a fairy."

Javaid grinned. "Truly?"

The boy nodded solemnly. "I never knew his name, but he was kind. He shared his bread."

Javaid didn't dare hope. There must be many boys with a sense of decency and hospitality, surely. But green eyes? "Where is this boy?"

"I do not know. I have not seen him for a time. Maybe he disappeared."

"Disappeared?" Javaid's echo was hollow and the boy shrugged.

"Boys disappear all the time. Try the teashops, just in case."

"Why?"

"I think he worked in one. A man called Kazim has a teashop. He saved him from a skewer."

Javaid's eyes nearly popped. "Is that what it sounds like?"

The boy narrowed his gaze at him, defensive now.

"Okay," Javaid said quickly. "Thank you for helping me."

He handed the boy the ten rupees. The boy looked around quickly before he whisked it under his qameez.

It took Javaid more than an hour to scour most of the teashops in the area. He even found a man called Kazim, but he hadn't heard of Razaq. He was on his way back to the main road when a boy caught him up.

"Excuse me, janab."

Javaid turned. He was tired; he had to go home and think of a better plan. "Yes?"

"I know a boy called Razaq. He was working for Kazim. You were at his restaurant."

"He said he didn't know a Razaq."

The boy didn't comment on that. "Razaq ran off. I am doing his shift."

"Was he from the mountains?"

"Ji, he said he was going to find his Uncle Javaid."

Javaid put both hands on the boy's shoulders. The boy flinched and Javaid let his arms drop. "Where did he say he was going?"

"Raja Bazaar."

"What is your good name?"

The boy hesitated. "You will not tell Kazim?"

"No."

"My name is Aslam, janab. Please find him. He knows nothing. He will be eaten up on the streets."

Chapter 10

"Why don't you find someone older to help with the work?" Razaq asked Zakim the next night after the children had fallen asleep.

"I work alone. Anyone else you have to pay in more ways than money." He shifted and recrossed his legs. "Everyone on this dump is in someone else's debt. If the bear doesn't earn enough, his landlord whips him."

"How have you survived without protection?" Razaq thought of the khans in the mountains. His father was a free man, but he had to give allegiance to the khan, give him a portion of the crops and fight for him if asked.

"I won't pay the price of that protection," Zakim said.

"They want money?"

Zakim scowled. "The bear wants Moti. Would you give Moti to pay off a monster?"

Razaq shook his head, yet he thought of boys like Aslam. How many children were payments for some debt? How many parents had no choice?

Zakim went on, "The landlord would sell her nath utarwai to the highest bidder—some wealthy fat *pig*." He spat out the swearword and Razaq blanched.

"Why is taking out her nose ring bad?" he ventured, knowing the word "nath" meant "nose ring."

Zakim glanced at him. "You don't know much. Nath utarwai means the first time she is with a man."

Razaq thought of Feeba waiting to be married to him because she was only twelve. "But Moti is too young."

He was shocked at the anger in Zakim's eyes. "There are too many bad men. Their minds are dirty."

Ardil's face flashed into his mind. Had he been sold to pay a debt? Surely not. It was said the khan's friend was helping the family.

"Why do you live here like this?" Razaq asked.

Zakim shrugged. "I have nowhere else."

"And Moti? Hira? Why do you pick up little girls?"

Zakim stared out the shelter's opening. Finally he said, "Something happened to my baby sister. My mother couldn't look after her, and she left her in the street, hoping a rich lady would take her. My mother died soon after, and I made a vow to find my sister."

"In this big city?"

A groan escaped Zakim. It was so ragged and intimate that Razaq glanced away. "I know I will never find my real sister, but Moti is her, so is Hira. And any others that I find." He stared at Razaq as if daring him to challenge him.

"And Raj?"

"I found him here in the scrap yard, wrapped in a shawl. He must have been thrown out for dead, but he was still alive."

Razaq didn't say anything for a long time. He listened to the sound of the traffic down the main bazaar, the train, shouts in the distance. All so different from the quiet nights he was used to. Then he said, "Don't the children need a mother?" He could see his own mother making the food each day and hear how she scolded him and told him what to do. She told stories at night—stories her mother must have told her, about wolves and monkeys, for she had never been to a madrasah like Uncle Javaid.

"That would be good, but Moti bosses them around like a mother already, and she has never known hers."

Razaq smiled. "Motherhood must be instinctive."

"Chup, quiet." Zakim snuffed out the candle with his fingers.

"What is it?"

Zakim whispered, "I heard a noise."

Razaq was amazed. He could usually hear if a jackal was creeping up on his goats in the night, but here? How could Zakim hear a noise among the clamor from the streets?

Zakim crouched by the doorway. Razaq saw the glint of his blade in the moonlight and felt for his own knife. He crawled out of the house box after Zakim. The attack was so sudden they weren't ready. Something smashed into Razaq's head from behind and he landed on the ground. He tried to clear his eyes but they blurred. He wiped them and looked up. He saw a figure silhouetted against the night sky lit by streetlights. He looked massive. Zakim had spoken truly: Nasir Ali was a bear.

If Nasir were a jackal, Razaq would know what to do. He would keep upwind and creep closer until he was near enough to shoot. Before he had a gun, he had used his slingshot. He could fell a jackal at twenty paces. Then he finished it off with his knife.

"Get up, you babies," Nasir said. His voice was a growl. "I'll beat you to a pulp."

Razaq stood. His head was still spinning. He saw Zakim front up to Nasir and smash his fist into his face. Nasir grunted and lifted Zakim as if he were a child. Zakim headbutted him and Nasir threw him to the ground.

"Is that the best you can do?"

Both boys rushed him. Razaq punched him in the middle, but it was as if they were toothless dogs attacking a bear. Nasir cuffed Razaq, and he flew back five paces.

Then a sleepy voice came from the box shelter. "What is happening?" It was Moti.

"Stay away!" Zakim's voice sounded like a whip cracking, but Moti kept coming.

"What are you doing?"

"Moti! Go back."

But she was too close. It all happened so quickly. Nasir gave a laugh like a bark and grabbed her. Moti screamed.

Razaq knew what would come next: Nasir would hurt Moti if they attacked him. Moti would render them powerless. One moment he saw Moti, and the next she shimmered into Seema, Seema when she was chased by a wild boar last year. It was Razaq who had shot it before it reached her.

He leaped onto Nasir's back, his knife ready, and squeezed his arms around Nasir's neck. He pulled tighter and the knife edged closer to Nasir's face. Nasir staggered. He had Moti under one arm and pulled at Razaq with the other, but Razaq held the blade to his cheek. "Let her go."

"I can kill you both." But Nasir's words were wheezy; Razaq's left hand was tightening on his windpipe.

"Try it. I will cut your throat."

Nasir dropped Moti and threw up both his arms. He grabbed hold of Razaq and tried to drag him off. At the same time, he pulled at his shalwar pocket. Zakim slammed a fist into Nasir's stomach in the instant that Razaq lost control of his knife. It sliced down Nasir's face. Nasir yelled and clutched his eye socket with both hands. Blood poured down his cheek.

Razaq slid to the ground as Zakim pressed the tip of his knife to Nasir's throat. "This is what you'll get if you bother us again."

Nasir backed away. Razaq knew the bigger boy could have overpowered them, but the cut must have unnerved him.

"He'll probably lose his eye," Zakim said. "We won't have tuklief from him for a while."

"Here, this is yours." Razaq held out a knife. "He must have been so sure he could win, it was still in his pocket."

Zakim stood for a second staring at Razaq, then grasped him close. Nothing else was said. Mountain men were the same. They might not always say what they felt, but the gratitude was evident in their actions.

Zakim lifted Moti and held her close as all three of them entered the Rag Mahal.

Chapter 11

Razaq was in the dump working, with Hira on his back pointing out good garbage, when Moti found him. "Your friend is here," she told him.

Razaq turned and saw Aslam. He didn't know what to say at first. Aslam was one person he had never thought to see again so soon.

"How did you find me?" he asked.

"Zakim heard me asking for you in Moti Bazaar."

Zakim walked up toward them. "He has good news for you, Chandi."

Razaq couldn't read Zakim's expression. He didn't have his usual grin.

"What is it?" he said to Aslam.

Aslam cleared his throat. "I know where your uncle is. He has come looking for you."

For a long moment Razaq was silent. Then he said, "Is he at Kazim's?"

Aslam's hesitation before he nodded was slight, but Razaq saw it was enough to make Zakim narrow his gaze at him.

Zakim drew Razaq aside. "Does he speak truly?"

Razaq slipped Hira to the ground and faced Zakim. "I believe so and if I go, my uncle will help you. Find a home for you and Moti and the others." He laid a hand on Hira's head.

Zakim lifted his chin. "You must do what you have to. If I had an uncle who wanted me, I would go to him."

"But you would take the children, too," Razaq said. He took a step forward and clasped Zakim to him in the kind of embrace mountain men gave a friend of their heart. "I will come back," he said when the hug was finished.

Zakim glanced at Aslam then back to Razaq. "May your eyes be bright." Then he grinned. "Jao, go. Live your life well. We will live ours."

❋

Razaq followed Aslam to the main road, where Aslam flagged a bus. "How is it Kazim let you come?" Razaq asked.

Aslam didn't meet his eyes. "He does not know where I am."

"Then we must hurry."

Just before they got off the bus, Aslam said, "Do not tell Kazim about your uncle. It is only me who knows who he is."

Razaq nodded. "Teik hai, fine." Then he said, "But isn't my uncle waiting there?"

"Come." Aslam ignored the question as the bus stopped at the adda. He ran toward Kazim's restaurant; Razaq close behind.

After all this time, Razaq was to see Uncle Javaid at last. He slowed as they drew closer to the small building. He couldn't see any men who looked like his uncle sitting outside. "Is my uncle still here?" he said.

Aslam beckoned for him to hurry.

Just as they were yards from the outside tables, Kazim rushed out. He grabbed Razaq and dragged him inside. "Good work," he said to Aslam. "Now get the naan."

Razaq stared after Aslam's back. Had he seen his uncle or not?

Kazim pulled Razaq into the cooking room. "What do you mean by running from your job? And stealing my thirty rupees? Where is it?"

Razaq shook his head. He didn't like the look on Kazim's face. He was in for a beating, he could tell.

"Gone, is it?" Kazim gave him a shake. "That's longer it will take to pay off your debt to me."

He took a bamboo stick from the wall. Razaq couldn't escape: Kazim was standing between him and the doorway. "This will teach you to obey me." He raised his arm and brought the stick down on Razaq's back and didn't stop.

Razaq's father had once made him eat stick, as he called it, when Razaq had let a wolf take a young goat, but it wasn't like this. Razaq fell to the floor and curled into a ball, steeling himself for each blow. He didn't know when they stopped.

When he woke, he found himself on his blanket, lying on his belly. He turned over and cried out.

Aslam was there with a bucket of water and a cloth. "You have to be washed so the cuts can heal." He helped Razaq peel off his shirt, pulling it from the new scabs. Razaq couldn't stop crying.

"You are lucky he went easy on you," Aslam said. "He does not want to mark you."

Once Aslam had finished rinsing his back, Razaq asked, "Has he done this to you?"

"Once. I ran away in the first week. He said if I ran again, he would beat my little brother. He even knew his name."

"My uncle wasn't here, was he?"

Aslam didn't answer. Instead, he said, "Kazim said if I didn't come back with you, he would cut my sister's face and sell her to a chakla, a brothel." He dribbled more water on Razaq's back. "She is ten years old."

Razaq clenched his fists. If anyone had hurt his sisters, he would have fought them, but what could Aslam do against Kazim? Aslam's fear made him an untrustworthy ally. Razaq wondered if he would be that powerless if his sisters were alive and lived within Kazim's reach. Yet was he any better off? He had told Zakim he would return. His father always said a mountain man's word was his honor. How could he prove that now?

Chapter 12

Javaid was sure Waqar wouldn't give him more time off to find Razaq. He would have to search in his lunch hour and after work. Raja Bazaar was like a huge rambling village. Where could he start?

He took a rickshaw down there during his lunch break and asked in shops along the main road. It was useless, of course. Shopkeepers looked at him as if he was crazy when he asked about Razaq. One man even asked him how he expected to find one boy in a bazaar as big as this. "A pin is hard to see in the dark," he said.

Javaid returned to the cloth shop but his heart wasn't in his work as it usually was. He half-listened to a conversation between the young worker, Zaid, and a customer as he keyed in the shop's takings. The customer was complaining about beggars.

"There are so many, even more now after the earthquake. Something should be done."

"Do you like this color?" Zaid said. "What can be done about the beggars, janab?"

Javaid frowned; Zaid sounded bored.

"The government should provide a camp for them so they don't bother us in the city," the customer said.

Javaid held his tongue, but wondered how the man would feel if it were his relatives being forced to the city for work.

Zaid threw out a bolt of blue cloth so it billowed over the counter. "This one," he said. "Your wife would look heavenly in it."

The bearded man frowned at him and Zaid realized what he'd said. "Not that I have seen her, of course, but I am sure she is—" He shut up about wives as Waqar made a cutting motion with his finger under his neck and turned to Javaid instead. "Ji, those beggars from up north. They have been in Moti Bazaar, too. Just think, one even asked for you by name, Javaid. The cheek to find out your name."

Javaid jumped up so fast the keyboard teetered on the desk. "When?"

Zaid's mouth slackened. "A few days ago. Just before you returned to work."

"What did he look like?" Javaid bent closer.

Zaid shrank back against the cloth shelves. "Like any beggar— dirty, always asking."

"And?" Javaid was inches from Zaid's face.

"I can't remember.... Fair, ji, under all that dirt he was fair. Certainly a jungly wild boy from the earthquake."

"What did you say to him? Did you say I was here?"

Zaid smiled as if his reply would make Javaid happy. "Of course not, I sent him off. We get enough beggars."

Javaid thumped the counter and swore.

Zaid stared at him in shock. "There is something wrong, brother? What did I say?"

Waqar spoke from his desk in the front window. "Take the afternoon off, Javaid, but shut the computer down first. I'll expect you earlier tomorrow and every morning until you have made the hours up."

"Thank you."

Javaid picked up his lunch pack, collected his bike from the storeroom, and hurried out to the gali. He almost ran with his bike to the cloth shop next door, then the next. He asked at all the cloth shops he could see. It must have been Razaq. If he had asked for him at Fazal Clothing Emporium then he must have remembered Javaid worked in a cloth shop. Would Razaq have known the shop's name? Was Javaid wasting his time enquiring everywhere? Maybe Fazal's was the only shop Razaq had visited.

It was growing late by the time Javaid was near the main road. One man thought he remembered Razaq, though the boy might have been a beggar. Who remembered beggars or even took notice when they spoke? Javaid had done it himself: brushed them away without even looking into their eyes.

"Ji, a boy was here asking for someone," the man said. "He seemed different from the ordinary beggar working for a landlord. Can't remember his name now—one of those khans from the mountains. I offered him chowkidar work, but he didn't last the night. He was gone when I came in the morning. All he wanted was my food."

Javaid didn't like the man's leer, as if beggars were worthless, and he didn't ask any more questions. He sighed as he walked out onto Iqbal Road. Razaq could be anywhere by now. He jumped onto his bike and pedaled to the police station.

❋

Javaid had no satisfaction with the police. The officer he spoke to refused even to fill out a First Information Report.

"You should have come here as soon as it happened," he said.

"But I didn't know then he was missing."

The officer shook his head. "There are too many missing children. And soon they return home after we have spent much expense. The parents only come to us as a last resort." He put his head to one side. "Now if he had been kidnapped, that is a different matter. Then we can fill out a pakka report."

"Actually, I think he was kidnapped."

"You think?"

Javaid thought of the money Auntie Latifa had received. Was it kidnapping if the abductor gave money?

The officer sighed noisily. "Where did this happen?"

"In Kala Dhaka."

The officer put down his pen. "That is not a government-controlled region."

"But he has been brought here to Rawalpindi."

"Does he have a birth certificate?"

Javaid tightened his mouth. "Probably not. They don't always register births in the mountains."

"Then how can we help you if the child has no legal record? There are many children like this and only 2 percent are ever being recovered." He held his thumb and forefinger together to show how little 2 percent was. "I shall put it in the Roznamcha, the daily diary, but keep searching, janab. You are the boy's only hope."

Javaid had trouble fighting a desire to punch the officer's lazy fat face.

He went to the local mosque next. The imam was solicitous. He waggled his head in sympathy. "So many children forced into bondage. We will broadcast his name and pray this evil will stop. May Allah be merciful to your nephew."

Chapter 13

After a few days, Razaq was set to washing dishes again on the night shift. Kazim yanked him to his feet, and Razaq was sure the cuts on his back reopened.

"Up you get, you lazy shaitan," Kazim said. "Be thankful you only had a light beating." He brought his head down to speak in Razaq's face. Razaq could see spit in the corners of his mouth. "But if you try that again, it will be worse. Do you understand?"

Razaq nodded. Kazim pushed him to the water trough to start washing cups.

He was not allowed outside. Kazim gave him an old ghee tin to do his business in, and Aslam had to dump it in the drain. Aslam ran for the naan all the time now, and Razaq cut vegetables in the afternoon. He thought it could have been worse. At least he'd had his clothes on during the beating and it was just a stick. Imagine if it had been a whip. He had seen a man in the mountains stripped and whipped by the order of the jirga council. After twenty lashes, the man's back was reduced to red mush, like overripe watermelon. It had taken him six weeks to get to his feet.

The days turned into a week and then another. Razaq tried to remember his life in the mountains: looking after the goats, sheep, and Peepu on the terraced slopes; the jobs he did with Seema and Layla. His mother's eyes, ringed with green, flashed into his head, reminding him to do a good job, to bring honor to the family. How could he do that here? His father's honor would require him to kill Kazim. That was what his father would do. He would kill Kazim and set his son free. Razaq sighed. He was too tired to run away. When his strength built up he would try again, and this time he wouldn't fall for stories from people like Aslam.

Then, a surprising thing happened. One afternoon, Kazim told Razaq to have a rest. That evening, he said Razaq could help wait on the tables. It was a break from washing dishes and gave him a chance to watch the TV. It was amazing how one afternoon's rest made Razaq feel almost chirpy. He set the plates of rice and bowls of curry on the tables and smiled at a man who was staring at him. If Kazim let him do this regularly, he would regain his strength in no time at all. Then he could find his uncle.

By ten, most of the customers had gone but one man remained. He wore an expensive suit coat over his shalwar qameez and had a gold watch on his wrist and a gold chain as thick as a halter around his neck. His shoes were made of green leather.

"Do you want more chai?" Razaq asked him in Urdu.

"No, get me Kazim," the man said without taking his eyes from Razaq.

Kazim must have heard because he hurried over, wiping his hands on a cloth. "You see what I mean?" he said to the man.

The man gave little away in his face, and Razaq wondered what Kazim meant.

"How much?" the man said.

Kazim spread his hands to encompass his poor restaurant. "One hundred and fifty thousand rupees."

The man chuckled. "You would match Ali Baba, you rogue. Only militants ask that much." Then his face changed into hard lines. "I'll give you a lakh, and nothing more." He stood and handed Kazim a piece of paper.

Kazim examined it. "It is good?"

"As good as the boy."

Razaq looked at Kazim, alarmed. Was it happening again? One lakh was a hundred thousand rupees, enough money to build many houses in the mountains. Why was the man giving all that money to Kazim?

Kazim pushed Razaq into the other room. "Get your things."

"What is happening?"

"I can't be worrying, waiting for when you'll run again. Mr. Malik has a good opportunity for you. If you do what you're told, you'll have a good life." Kazim grinned and Razaq shrank from the greed in his eyes. "I knew you would bring a fortune for me."

Kazim went back to Mr. Malik.

"I told you he was biding his time," Aslam said, "just waiting for the right customer."

"But I cannot be sold again."

"If I was as pretty as you, it would have been me. At least you will get good food and maybe a TV. A ride in a car sometimes."

"What do you know?" Razaq said. "Where am I going?"

"Mr. Malik is a dala. He trains boys and girls for business."

Razaq paled.

"Hurry up. Mr. Malik is leaving." Kazim's voice from the outside room sounded jaunty.

"You have to help me," Razaq whispered, but Aslam merely shrugged.

"What can any of us do? Mr. Malik is a big businessman with many people working for him. No one crosses him."

Razaq put on his pakol, the green jacket, and his father's sandals. He put the empty purse in his pocket. He walked to the door—there was no escaping.

Mr. Malik smiled at him, but it didn't reach his eyes as smiles were meant to. "Come, beta. We have much to do. The first thing will be to give you a proper bath. Then we shall see what we have."

He looked as if finding out what he had was going to be pleasant, but Razaq only felt ill.

✤

Razaq stared out of the car window. Lights flashed into his eyes as they turned corners. The cinema, bright with lights and painted billboards of half-naked actresses and heroes caked with blood and mud, lit up a whole block. Hundreds of men stood around in the streets. It looked as if the city never slept. It should have been exciting—this was his first ride in a car—but the thought of what might happen to him stole his joy. He had already tried the door handle, but it was locked. Mr. Malik sat in the front seat next to the driver, and Razaq caught him glancing at him in the rearview mirror. He had a small smile at the corner of his mouth that made Razaq more worried.

The car pulled up outside a house with high white walls made of cement. There were numbers on the gate. When Razaq was ushered inside the house, he saw there were many rooms. They walked down a hallway, past a room where children were still awake and watching TV. The place looked like a fancy madrasah and Razaq's spirits lifted a little. Perhaps Aslam was wrong; maybe he could learn some more English words here. If he didn't like this job, he could find another. Razaq stopped himself and thought of Kazim's restaurant. That wasn't really a job—how long had it taken him to work that out? Too long. He probably wouldn't have escaped from Kazim again, but was he any better off now? He wasn't sure. Mr. Malik had paid much money—would he be more strict?

Razaq glanced up at Mr. Malik's face: it looked hard, like sunbaked mud. He walked tall, his back straight like an army general's, his hands big. *What are those hands capable of*, Razaq wondered.

"This is where we will start, my mountain prince," Mr. Malik said.

Razaq looked into the room. It held a huge white trough with taps. He stared at it, uncomprehending, and Mr. Malik chuckled.

"It is called a bath. No doubt you washed in a river?"

Razaq nodded.

"Here we can capture water. We can capture anything in the city."

He looked at Razaq as if he was thinking he could even capture boys like him. Razaq gritted his teeth. He was sure they would drown him in that bath—he couldn't swim— and he kept his feet rooted to the floor. Mr. Malik called out and immediately two people rushed into the room. One was a young man, as tall and heavy looking as Nasir Ali but quicker on his feet, and the other was a woman.

"Bathe him," Mr. Malik said. "Bring him to me when he is ready."

Razaq fought valiantly, but the young man was so much bigger and the woman surprisingly strong. It wasn't long before his clothes were stripped off and he was in the bath with only his tarveez on, being soaped and scrubbed with a tough brush.

"Ow."

The woman grunted. "It will hurt more if you struggle. Hold him, Murad." Then she murmured, "This one will be trouble. Already he has been beaten, but it seems it hasn't worked."

Razaq tried to pull his arms away from Murad's grasp to cover himself, but Murad was too strong. Never before, not since he was a tiny child, had Razaq been completely naked. The shame daunted him, then suddenly the scrubbing was over.

"A jao, come out," the woman said. "The boss will be pleased with you, I expect, but do what he says." She picked up a towel and roughly wiped him. "Do not let his nice words fool you."

With that piece of advice given, she kneeled to clean out the bath and Murad twisted Razaq's arms behind his back and pushed him toward the door.

Razaq turned his head toward the woman. "My clothes."

"You can't put those filthy things back on, you'll get dirty again," the woman said.

Murad gave him another shove into the hallway. To Razaq's relief, no one else was there to see him naked. He couldn't hear the TV so maybe the children had gone to bed. He was pushed into a room on the left where Mr. Malik and another man were drinking chai from glass cups.

"So." Mr. Malik turned as Razaq entered. He raised a hand slightly and Murad disappeared. Razaq glanced behind him at the doorway. How far was it? Perhaps he could run.

"Don't even think about it," Mr. Malik said. "Kazim told me he had to beat you, but I see he hasn't broken your spirit. That is good." He took another sip of tea while Razaq tried to cover his front. "Now that Farida has given you a bath, I see you are even fairer than I thought." He looked at the other man who inclined his head and smiled. "I think I have hit the target this time, do you not agree, Bashir?"

"Zarur, certainly." The other man finally spoke.

Razaq stared at him in surprise. He spoke like a mountain man, but he wasn't dressed like one.

"Tell us about yourself, prince of the mountains." Mr. Malik put a biscuit in his mouth. Razaq watched him slowly chewing. When had he last eaten?

"Hungry? Here." Mr. Malik passed the plate and Razaq hesitated. Would he be allowed to take one? "Khao, eat," Mr. Malik said.

Razaq reached out and popped one in his mouth. It was such a long time since he had eaten anything so sweet. His father had brought biscuits home from the village one day when Uncle Javaid and Auntie Amina had visited. His cousin Sakina was still a little child toddling around their one-roomed house. He had picked her up, given her a biscuit, and shown her the goats. Seema and Layla came, too. The three little girls had shrieked with laughter at everything Razaq did. It had been a good day.

"Beta, what was life like in the mountains?"

Razaq didn't like Mr. Malik calling him "son." The shop owner who had said he could be a chowkidar had called him that, too, yet he must have known slavers would come in the night. How much would the man have been paid, he wondered.

Mr. Malik flicked at a fly and Razaq said, "Accha hai."

"Accha? Just good? What did you do?"

Mr. Malik looked impatient and Razaq remembered Farida's warning. "I looked after goats, our sheep, fetched water. Helped Abu grow grain, my mother to grow vegetables."

"Did you go to school?"

"Sometimes." No need for them to know he could read and write a little.

Mr. Malik appraised him. "You look about twelve or thirteen."

Razaq stayed silent. Some instinct made him let the men think he was younger than fourteen.

Mr. Malik sighed. "Have you ever been with a man?"

Razaq thought of Ardil. Was it like this for him? Then he remembered Saleem. If Kazim hadn't saved him, he may have a different story to tell. He shook his head and the two men smiled at him. The warmth from the bath was wearing off. Didn't the men know he was cold, or was this their way of showing him who was boss?

Mr. Malik called and Murad appeared. "Take him to the room." Then he said to Razaq, "Have a good rest, beta. Tomorrow we shall see what you are good at, and you can start your training in your new job. We have no goats and sheep to look after here in Islamabad, but there are many things you can do. Can you dance?"

Razaq lifted his chin in affirmation.

"Then we shall see."

Murad took Razaq to a room down the hall. There was a bed with a folded white shalwar qameez on it. Razaq pulled on the shalwar with relief. Then Murad pushed him toward a small adjoining room. In it was a white seat. Razaq stood looking at it until Murad shoved him aside, untied his own shalwar, and peed in it. Then he pushed a shiny button on top and water flushed his pee away. Realization dawned: it was a toilet. Razaq remembered his uncle telling him about them.

"How long have you been here?" he asked Murad, but he was met with a stony silence. Razaq realized with a jolt that Murad would not be his friend.

Chapter 14

Razaq woke to his first day at the white house, as he thought of it. Everything was white: the room he slept in, the bath and the room it was in, even the walls. Murad marched him to another room with a table and benches, not unlike Kazim's restaurant. Aslam was right about the food: there were parathas and puri halva and chai. There was plenty on the plate, too; Razaq hadn't eaten so well since before the earthquake.

The children he had seen watching TV the night before sat around the table. There were six, and all seemed younger than Razaq. Most looked about twelve. One of them was a girl. Razaq stole a look at her. She was very pretty with big eyes the color of almonds. Would Feeba have looked like that, he wondered. The children seemed happy enough, although a few looked tired. Maybe Aslam had been wrong and this was a proper job, or a place that looked after fatherless children. Yet Mr. Malik didn't seem like a religious man intent on doing good deeds.

After breakfast, a man came to the house carrying a tabla, a pair of hand drums. With him was a woman. She was tall and looked much like the woman who had pinched Razaq's cheek in Moti Bazaar. They went into the room with the TV. The children followed them in and Razaq brought up the rear, curious. The pretty girl spoke to him but he couldn't understand her words. She switched to Urdu.

"It is our dancing lesson," she said. "Those people are from Qasai Gali."

The name meant nothing to Razaq. "What language were you speaking?" he asked.

"Punjabi," she said. "Punjab is where I come from." Her face clouded before she asked, "Where are you from?"

"Kala Dhaka, the Black Mountains."

"Where is that?"

"In Khyber Pukhtunkhwa. I am a Pukhtun and that is the language I speak. My grandmother spoke Hindko so I understand that also."

Her eyes widened.

"How did you learn Urdu?" he asked.

"In school." She said it as if it was obvious.

Razaq stared at her. His sisters never went to school. Nor Feeba. But he was glad this girl had.

The woman called the girl's name. "Tahira."

Razaq said the name softly and curled his tongue around the way it sounded in his mouth.

The tabla player started up a rhythm and Tahira raised her arms to dance. Razaq thought she was magical. She turned her head and made her hands tell a story. Her feet tapped on the ground. Razaq could almost hear bells even though she wore none.

Just then the woman stopped her and said, "Do it like this, beti." She showed Tahira what to do with her eyes. Razaq stared at the woman. He had never heard a woman speak with such a deep voice, even deeper than the lady's who had pinched his cheek.

Tahira danced again and the younger children clapped in rhythm. A louder clapping came from the doorway as Tahira finished. Razaq glanced behind him and saw Mr. Malik smiling at Tahira. She sank to the floor, looking happy to have danced, but Razaq frowned. Mr. Malik's smile was disturbing. Were they all in the house just to be fed well and have expensive dancing lessons?

"Shahbash, shahbash. Well done," Mr. Malik said. "You are a true princess, little one." His gaze shifted to Razaq. "Now let us see what our mountain prince can do."

He motioned to the tabla player and flicked his fingers at Razaq to dance. The beat wasn't familiar, but Razaq held his arms out and danced the steps the men performed at weddings in the mountains. He lifted his feet as if he were dancing between crossed swords. At first he felt self-conscious, but as he turned he saw Tahira watching him. It was her he wanted to impress, not Mr. Malik.

When the tabla stopped, she smiled at him. He was astonished to find her smile was worth everything, even being caged in the white house.

"Shahbash." Mr. Malik's praise wasn't quite as effusive as it had been for Tahira. "Can you do something with him, Pretty?" he asked the dance instructor.

"Certainly, sahib."

Mr. Malik's cell phone rang, and he walked down the hallway talking.

Pretty spent the rest of the morning training the children how to dance for an audience. One dark-skinned boy danced in a colored shalwar and a tiny silk vest. If he made a mistake he giggled, but mostly he did very well.

"Danyal, concentrate," Pretty said, but she didn't sound angry. Even Razaq smiled when Danyal looked at him and rolled his eyes.

When the dancing class was over, the children gathered again in the room with the table and Farida brought in a bowl of chicken curry and chapattis. Razaq had only ever had chicken at weddings. If they got food again in the evening, it would be three times Razaq had eaten that day. He was lucky to eat twice a day at Kazim's and that wasn't just because of Ramadan. He wondered if they were being plumped up like chickens ready for the market.

Danyal sat beside him. "Ramadan finished last night so this is our Eid-ul-Fitr feast. Mr. Malik lets Farida spoil us every now and then." He grinned.

Razaq was astounded that he hadn't realized what day it was. His thoughts had been consumed with being brought to Mr. Malik's house. At home, his mother would have made new clothes for him and his sisters, a new sweater maybe. Sometimes there was a gift, like his grandfather's gun his father gave him at his eleventh Eid. Or his new lambswool hat when he was twelve.

"Shall we go outside and play a game after this?" Razaq said to Danyal. "Do you have a soccer ball?"

The smile disappeared from Danyal's face. "We do not go outside." He looked over his shoulder before he said, "All the doors have special security codes. There is no way out."

That afternoon, no one was in the hallway and Razaq thought he'd test Danyal's statement. There had to be a way out; he just had to discover it. He found the numbers by the front door that Danyal must have been talking about and pressed a few. They made a sound like the notes of a flute and Murad materialized as suddenly as a jinn and slapped Razaq's hand away from the buttons.

He hauled Razaq to Mr. Malik's room. Mr. Malik was still eating his curry. Razaq watched him dip the chapatti into the bowl and pop it into his mouth. His fingers were impeccably clean, so was his mustache. He pushed the dish away and Murad took it out while Mr. Malik smoothed both sides of his mustache with one finger.

"Now, my prince," Mr. Malik began. Razaq bit down on his annoyance. He was sick of being called a prince. He used to call the goat they fattened for Eid-ul-Adha a prince. "You cannot go outside in case you get lost. Islamabad is a big city with many evil people. Only Bashir, Murad, and myself know the combination so there is no point in trying." He studied Razaq. "I can see you need something to occupy you. Dancing is helpful to know, but you need to have a trade. A man has come to teach you how to give a malish, a massage. And then you will be a malishia."

He raised his eyebrows, but Razaq said nothing. Mr. Malik smiled at him. Razaq was wary of those smiles: he looked too much like a leopard licking its lips. "You don't know what a massage is, but you soon will. You can practice on me once you know how."

He flicked his head toward the door, and Razaq was surprised to see Murad there; he moved so silently. He took Razaq to the room he had slept in the night before, then disappeared without a word. Razaq thought he was the rudest person he had ever met.

A young man stood behind a chair in the middle of the room, a towel over his shoulder. "Sit here, please, Razaq, and take off your qameez. My name is Sunni. First we shall learn to do the head massage. The customer feels very relaxed after a head massage. Start with the shoulder like this."

Sunni proceeded to give Razaq a massage. Razaq was determined not to enjoy it, but with Sunni's fingers on his neck, then his scalp, stroking his forehead and then his temples, he was transported to a different place. He had seen barbers do something like this in the village bazaar, but he had never experienced it. His mother had always cut his hair.

Sunni gave him a clap on the back. "Accha, now it is your turn."

"What?"

"Now you do it to me."

"But I won't remember how to."

Sunni grinned. "I will talk you through it. Come. This is the best way to be learning."

And so Razaq began his training for his new job. The report to Mr. Malik stated Razaq showed great promise as a malishia, and Sunni became his instructor.

Chapter 15

Sometimes men came in the evenings, and the boys danced for them. Tahira wasn't included and Razaq thought how respectful of Mr. Malik to not show her to the men, for even though she was only twelve she was still a girl.

Apart from dancing classes and Sunni's massage training in the mornings, the afternoons were Razaq's own to fill as he wished. The TV was always on. He was becoming used to seeing people do things in that black box and remembering it was just a play.

The younger boys loved watching cartoons and movies with fighting in them. "Amir Khan," Danyal shouted, "here he is, he's the best." Razaq remembered how Aslam had liked him, too.

"You've never seen TV much?" Danyal asked him.

Razaq shook his head. "We didn't have it in the mountains."

"Ah, no reception," Danyal said wisely. Danyal seemed to know so much and yet he must have only been twelve. "Didn't you have a dish?"

Razaq frowned. "Enough dishes, of course."

Danyal hooted. "A satellite dish, you mountain goat."

Razaq squinted at him. "You are fortunate; if anyone like Murad called me a goat, I would fight him."

Once his father had called him a goral, a goat antelope, when he jumped from rock to rock chasing a sheep.

Danyal grinned, and in that instant he reminded Razaq of Zakim. "You are in luck then for Murad will never call you anything."

"Why not?"

"Has he said anything to you yet?"

"No."

"And he never will."

Realization dawned on Razaq. "He is a mute?"

"Hahn ji. Had his tongue chopped off. He can't write either, so he can never tell anyone about Mr. Malik's business, can he?"

Razaq stared at him.

Danyal wriggled his eyebrows up and down, then grinned again. "So be careful what you say." He made a sawing motion on his tongue and gagged. Danyal could always make Razaq smile.

❊

One afternoon, Razaq sat with Tahira in a corner while the boys watched Angrezi cartoons on the cable channel. She told him about her village. "We had a buffalo. I used to milk her."

"I used to milk goats," Razaq said.

She smiled. "I walked to the well with a can on my head. The buffalo turned the waterwheel to bring the water up."

"I filled buckets at a stream."

"Cheat."

He grinned at her. "Did you have goats?"

"A few. My father planted wheat, and we threshed it after harvest. That was fun, jumping on the stalks. My father had to give half the grain to the landlord." She fell quiet.

It sounded a lot like Razaq's own life—until the earthquake. "It was a terrible sound that came from the middle of the earth," he told her, "like nothing I've ever heard. And all my family died."

Tahira didn't say anything, but she leaned closer and put a hand over his. Razaq stared at her fingers curling around his and reminded himself she was just a child.

Razaq thought he heard Tahira call out that night. Had he imagined it? He listened a moment, then heard a sob. He crept down the hallway and found her alone in a room, weeping. Razaq didn't hesitate—he did what he would have for Seema or Layla if they woke up from a nightmare. He sat beside her and put his arm around her back. She let her head fall onto his shoulder.

"What is the matter?" he whispered. "You have a bad dream?"

She nodded and wiped her face with a shawl. She was only a few years older than Seema, but Razaq felt such a confusion of emotion that it unnerved him. He wanted to protect her as if she were his sister. Yet she was not his sister, and if anyone in the mountains saw him do this, they would both be punished. He managed to push those thoughts aside. It was different here. There would never have been an unrelated girl sleeping in his home.

"Can you tell me?" he said.

"It was fire." She sniffed. "I hate fire." She stopped and Razaq waited. "It is how my family died. My village was attacked. I had a brother, the same age as you. He tried to fight but a man shot him. It was Easter—our Eid—they burned the church. Almost every Christian in the village was inside."

Razaq stiffened. She was Christian?

"I was in the latrine," she went on. Razaq could hardly see her—just heard her small voice telling him these things. He didn't move his arm away. "It was Muslims from the next village who did it. Afterward, I wandered out to the main road and a man on a wagon picked me up. He seemed kind. I told him what had happened and he said it was justice because of the way America treats Muslims. I knew nothing of America, and I said what my father had told me: that we are all Pakistanis. But the man said true Pakistanis are only Muslim."

"I am a Muslim," Razaq said, wondering if she would hate him.

She turned her head. Could she see him? It was as if she was watching him, then she said softly, "But you wouldn't burn me."

"No." Razaq said it with more fervor than he meant to.

Tahira sighed. "Today was our big Eid, Christmas. No one knows about it here," she whispered, "they only know today as Ali Jinnah's birthday, but in our village it was the biggest day of the year. We had new clothes and colored sweet rice, like a wedding."

Razaq touched her face and knew that if he could see her eyes, he would find himself reflected in them. It was a place he wanted to stay forever.

❄

Sunni brought oil bottles on a metal rack for Razaq. "This one is made from coconut, mustard, and olive oil with some coriander. This one is saanda—it's from the fat of a lizard and it makes the customer very happy." He gave Razaq a wink, but Razaq didn't know what he meant.

Sunni showed him how to give a full massage, and soon, Mr. Malik said Razaq could start earning his keep. He was to have customers in his room while the younger boys were watching TV in the afternoons.

The first man that Murad directed to Razaq's room was tall. "Please lie on the bed," Razaq said, putting a towel where the man's head would rest. He started on the man's shoulders.

"That feels good," the man said. "What else can you do—full body massage?"

Razaq glanced at the man's long legs and feet, thinking it would take all afternoon. "Yes, if you want."

The man rolled over and stood up. "Why don't we cut the crap? Just bend over the bed, and I'll massage you."

Razaq saw the same look in the man's eyes as Saleem had had that day when he'd grabbed him in the gali. "No."

He ran out of the room and bumped into a hard wall of flesh. It was Murad. He sent Razaq flying into the doorjamb, belted him across the head twice, and dragged him down the hall to Mr. Malik.

The customer followed them, tying his shalwar cord. "I want my money back."

Mr. Malik was in the doorway with money in his hand when the man reached him. He gave the man the money between two fingers. "Come back tomorrow. He is just playing hard to get." He winked and, miraculously, the man grinned.

Mr. Malik did not smile at Razaq. "Bring him in here." It was a growl and his face had grown dark. "Show him what the customer wanted."

This time Razaq had no choice but to lean over the table, and Murad's iron arm kept him there. This time there

111

was no Kazim to save him. Now he knew what Ardil had endured and why he had never told. Razaq tried not to cry out, but his mouth bled from biting the inside of his cheek. When it was done, he stood unsteadily in front of Mr. Malik. Both men ignored the trickle Razaq could feel running down his legs.

"I am afraid Sunni's education has been remiss," Mr. Malik said. "He didn't show you everything. From now on if a customer asks what you do, you say 'massages.' If they ask what else, you say 'whatever you want.' It is double for whatever they want. Understand?"

Razaq swallowed.

"Understand?"

Razaq finally opened his mouth. "Ji."

"This way you will pay off your debt to me sooner. I will put aside some money for you—twenty-five rupees each massage, fifty rupees for 'whatever they want.' Much better that you work for me than be on the streets getting diseases. Samajti hai, do you understand this, Razaq?"

Razaq fought the tears that were pooling in his eyes and nodded.

"Sunni will come for an extra session in the morning and tell you all you need to know." His mouth tightened as if he had some extra words to say to Sunni. He waved Razaq away.

If Murad hadn't pushed Razaq down the hall to his room, he wouldn't have been able to walk. For the rest of the afternoon he lay on his bed, wishing the throbbing would go away. But he knew that when the pain had gone there would be a different pain—that of shame. Nothing washed that away.

Men in the mountains said that badil, revenge, could erase shame, but Razaq wasn't so sure. Would he feel better if he could kill Murad? Wouldn't he then feel shame for killing?

The next afternoon, the man returned. He smiled at Razaq as if it was all a game, a game he was pleased to play. "Come on, pretty boy, show me your love."

Razaq turned around while the man untied his shalwar. He ground his teeth and tried not to think of his mother's horror if she knew what was happening to him, or how his father would avenge him if he were alive. He would call this "whatever" from now on, even though it was still skewering. Perhaps his mind would cope with it better.

※

After that day, Razaq watched the other boys. Were they in the same situation as he was? As far as he knew, he was the only malishia in the house. Did the boys have visitors too or were they just learning to dance?

Razaq couldn't tell Tahira what had happened, though he suspected Danyal knew. He had watched Razaq sit carefully on the bench for his meal the evening after Murad's "lesson." Danyal always said Punjabi jokes were the best but that night he didn't tell any.

One thing Razaq was sure of: he wouldn't be doing this forever. He made some calculations. If Mr. Malik had paid one hundred thousand rupees for him and since Sunni had said the massages cost up to five hundred with "whatever," then he had to do two hundred to be free. If he did a few a free in three months.

dered what Mr. Malik had paid for Tahira. He to work a few more months for her freedom, too.

Chapter 16

The searching took so much of his time, but Javaid would not give up. For weeks now, he had kept asking in shops in Moti and Raja Bazaars, even though no one had ever seen Razaq. One Friday, Javaid took a bus to a nigeban, a shelter for runaway and lost boys that he saw listed on the Internet. It was an old cement house, bravely whitewashed. Javaid imagined the boys did it themselves.

A Mr. Mahmood took Javaid to his office, passing through a room where a young man was teaching the boys arithmetic.

"Here we teach the boys life skills for when they are ready to leave," Mr. Mahmood said. "We instill the importance of education. It is the only way to rise from the slums. We train them in simple trades also and try to get the older ones into jobs. And we give counseling."

He called softly to a boy near the back of the room. "Suneel." The boy came and stood in front of Mr. Mahmood. "This boy escaped from a carpet factory. He was sold into service to pay off a debt. He is afraid for his parents, of what the factory owner will do to them, but he saw his chance and ran. He cannot go home or his parents will be forced to return him."

Javaid smiled, but the boy dropped his gaze to his feet. Mr. Mahmood gave a silent command with his hand and the boy sat back on the carpet.

"He has made much progress," Mr. Mahmood said softly. "He had been abused in his workplace and is still wary of strange men." He pointed to another boy. "That one we found on the streets. He had lost his parents and was surviving by collecting rags and who knows what else. Before he came here, he was beaten and . . ."

He left the sentence hanging and Javaid felt the old fear uncurl in the pit of his stomach. What would Razaq be like when he found him? He remembered him as a clever and happy child, polite and eager to please. He had a highly protective streak and looked after his sisters and could shoot or trap any animal that threatened his goats. He had even saved one sister from a wild boar. All good attributes for surviving in the mountains, but would that resilience be enough to survive on the streets of a city? Or would he become a shadow like this boy from the carpet factory?

"I am looking for my nephew, Abdur-Razaq Nadeem Khan," he told Mr. Mahmood. "Has he come here?"

"I do not remember this name, but come into my office and I will check my records."

Javaid waited impatiently while Mr. Mahmood opened his ledger and put on his glasses. After some time he said, "I am sorry, I cannot help you." He looked up at Javaid and took off the glasses. "There are so many children in bondage. Many are missing, some ran away from home, others were abducted or tricked. There are so few workers and resources to free them. The government does what it can, but truly the responsibility for their escape has to rest with the children themselves. As with Suneel." He inclined his head toward the school room.

"I truly hope you find your nephew," Mr. Mahmood continued, then paused. "If you do not, please consider returning. Many of these boys need a home of their own. We can find a good match for you."

Javaid was appalled, but he thanked the man. "May God bless your work here."

"We survive by donations, janab. The government cannot give us much."

Javaid reached for his money. It was a good cause. Maybe his small donation would help some other boy find his family. Afterward, as he waited on the side of the road for the bus, he had to keep blinking away the tears.

Chapter 17

One evening, six men with suit coats over their shalwar qameezes visited the white house. They came separately, and when they'd all arrived, Mr. Malik introduced them to the boys as uncles. One short man with long fingers had red leather shoes as fine as Mr. Malik's green ones. Another was very tall. They were not handsome men, but they looked clean and rich. They watched the younger boys dance to the tabla and harmonium. Then Mr. Malik did something very strange: he called for Tahira.

Razaq drew in a sharp breath as all the uncle-men sat straighter on the couches. The younger boys were sent to bed, but Razaq lingered in the hallway. Tahira looked like his Auntie Amina had when she was married, like Razaq imagined Feeba would have looked at their wedding. She wore a red and gold shalwar qameez, red glass bangles up her arms, even a gold pendant on her forehead, and makeup on her mouth and eyes. Farida had dressed Tahira like a bride.

Mr. Malik asked Tahira to dance. Tonight she wore ghungroo, bells. How they jingled; she was such a talented dancer. When the song had finished, Razaq heard the men begin bidding, just like Ikram had with Kazim. But there were six men this time and the bidding started at fifty thousand rupees. It looked as if they all liked Tahira's dancing.

"It will be the first time this little princess has danced alone for a man," Mr. Malik said.

"Are you sure?" Tall Uncle said.

"Certainly," Mr. Malik said, "Dr. Bahadur, MD Fail, has checked her."

The men looked satisfied.

"To dance for you personally alone," Mr. Malik prompted, and the bidding rose like a flock of birds into the sky.

Razaq had never heard such sums spoken before, and all to see Tahira dance. How beautiful they thought she was. For a moment, pride lifted in his heart. When she was older, he would marry her. Then, she would dance for him alone. In the mountains, no woman danced for a man unless he was her husband. Razaq's father would never have allowed Seema or Layla to dance for a male visitor. So it was very odd for Mr. Malik to show Tahira to other men. Razaq frowned. Although Mr. Malik called them uncles, Razaq didn't think the men were related to Mr. Malik at all. They all looked so different.

The bidding ended with Short Uncle saying four lakh. He said it with a squeak in his voice. There were sad sighs from the other men, but Short Uncle couldn't hide his triumph. He wrote on a piece of paper, then he led Tahira to a room down the hall. She gave Razaq a furtive glance as Short Uncle opened the door.

Razaq sat on the floor in the hallway to wait for Tahira's dancing to finish so he could congratulate her. He'd had no idea so much money could be made from dancing. Perhaps Ikram had been right about the soccer, too.

He heard the man's voice in a low murmuring—he must be telling her a story. Then he heard the bells Tahira wore. He closed his eyes, imagining the way she turned, her hands opening and closing to show the path of the story, her feet making the bells ring with joy. There was silence, another low murmur, an exclamation, then a shriek.

Razaq raced to the door and pounded on it. "Stop. What are you doing?"

Murad was there instantly, and as Razaq was dragged away, he could hear Tahira screaming his name.

❋

Razaq was beaten so badly he couldn't move until the next morning. On the way to breakfast, he passed Tahira's room. Farida was in there with a man who had a leather bag on the floor next to him. "She will heal," the man said. Razaq moved on before he was noticed, but he had seen Tahira's leg. There was blood on it.

Murad found him in the eating room and hauled him to Mr. Malik's room. As usual, Murad was not gentle and Razaq soon had new bruises from being banged into the wall on the way down the hall. Mr. Malik was drinking coffee with Bashir when Murad threw Razaq into the room. Razaq landed on his knees.

Mr. Malik didn't even put his cup down. "I am sorry you had to be beaten, but you cannot disturb my business," he said.

Razaq didn't think he looked sorry at all. He kept his mouth firmly shut in case he said what he thought.

Mr. Malik finished his coffee and looked at him closely. "So you want Tahira for yourself, is that it?"

Mr. Malik's voice sounded calm, but terror struck Razaq like a lightning bolt. In the mountains, a man could be killed for admitting such a thing. Yet Mr. Malik didn't have the look of righteous revenge mountain men wore when they were about to kill for honor. Razaq glanced at Murad standing by the door. He hadn't moved toward him on any unspoken command. Razaq forced himself to calm down.

"She is a sister to me," he said. It was almost the truth.

Mr. Malik kept regarding him, his head on one side. He tapped the side of his chair, his empty cup still in one hand. It was unnerving. Razaq chewed his bottom lip.

"We should have him fixed," Bashir said. "Bring back that failed medical student you use to check the kids."

Mr. Malik lifted his hand for silence. His gaze raked Razaq's face, and he tried not to flinch. "Tahira was untouched. Mr. Hamid was most pleased. He did say she was rather shy."

Bashir grinned. "He didn't seem to mind that."

Razaq clenched his fists. The anger felt better than fear. Tahira had no family to avenge her. Well, he would be her family now. Then a sobering thought struck him. In the mountains, she would be killed for being with a man who wasn't her husband, unless there were four witnesses to say she was forced. He knew it had happened, but he was underage. Perhaps he and Farida would count as one witness, and also Bashir. Mr. Malik and Murad knew, too, but they did nothing to help her. He tried to clear his eyes of the rage he was sure must show.

"Why don't we send him to France like that other bebekoof who gave us so much trouble?" Bashir continued.

Mr. Malik smiled his leopard grin. "This will work out for us. Just think, he will never run. We have found where his soft belly is at last. Tahira will control him." Then he said evenly to Razaq, "You will always do exactly as I say or it will go badly for Tahira."

Both men watched him as if checking what those words would do to him.

Razaq said, "Soon I will have paid my debt to you and then I will pay Tahira's."

The men's faces dropped a moment in astonishment and then Mr. Malik threw back his head and laughed. "It will take you many years to pay off your debt to me and hers. Do you know how much she's worth?"

Ji, four lakh, Razaq thought but didn't say. He would work years for her if he had to.

Mr. Malik turned to Bashir. "We have a new shipment coming in a few weeks. It is time to put Tahira to work. Mrs. Mumtaz has space at the moment."

Bashir raised his eyebrows. "I thought she only took family members—trying to act like the old high-class kanjar families who ran brothels. Does she provide music?"

"She's branching out," Mr. Malik said. "She's taken a chance setting up in that gali, but I'm backing her."

"And him?" Bashir inclined his head toward Razaq.

"He will go, too," Mr. Malik said, as if that had been his plan all along. "He can give massages there as well as here, but," he addressed Razaq directly, "Mrs. Mumtaz will take no nonsense. She'll cut you herself if you give her any trouble."

It was three days before Tahira came to breakfast. She sat stiffly on the bench and stared at the table. Razaq pushed a paratha over to her, and she took it without looking up. That first morning she said nothing, but in the afternoon Razaq found her in the dancing room.

"I am sorry," he said. "I could have stopped it."

"No one could have stopped it," she said.

"I thought it was just dancing. If I'd known . . ."

She looked at him then, with eyes as lifeless as glass. "It *was* a dance and that is how I will think of it. I used to love dancing; now I hate it."

"I will work to pay off your debt. Mr. Malik said he will put aside money each time I . . ." he faltered, ". . . do a massage."

Tahira's face showed the sort of pity given to someone who is younger and doesn't yet understand the world. "That wagon man who picked me up sold me to a man in a black turban with a huge gun. I was thrown into a room with other children. We were fed once a day, and after a week I was sold as domestic help to a big house here in Islamabad." How bleak she sounded. "I cleaned the house and washed dishes for two years. Then the son of the house started talking to me while I was dusting. I thought I would get into trouble and I was right. His mother caught him and said I had to go. I wasn't the right age any more for their family. She put me in a rickshaw and the driver dumped me on the street at one of the markets. I managed to keep away from the men there and met a boy who showed me a safe place to sleep in a gali. He patted my head and said I was pretty like his sister. Later, I found out he worked for Mr. Malik. It only took Mr. Malik a day to find me. He said he would take me to a safer place and promised me a room in his house and dancing lessons.

But he didn't tell me everything." She shook her head sadly at Razaq. "He will never let us go. I know that now. I thought he loved me as a true uncle, that he might adopt me, but he doesn't love me at all. I have been a fool."

Razaq didn't know what to say to comfort her. Not when he also wanted someone to tell him how to make sense of it all.

Chapter 18

Two weeks later, Murad took Razaq and Tahira out to the car. It was night, and they had no idea where they were going. Razaq was pushed into the back, next to Tahira.

"This is the second time I've been in a car," he whispered. Tahira nodded. "Me, too."

The driver was the same man who had brought Razaq to the white house—how long ago? Razaq wasn't sure. A few months? The driver glanced at them in the mirror. Razaq wondered what he was thinking. Did he know about his boss's business? Razaq knew now what that business was: enslaving children and making money from them. Wasn't Mr. Malik educated enough to have a proper job?

The driver spoke. "You kids watch yourselves in the Qasai Gali. Lots of china shops there now, but they say it used to be full of chaklas, brothels. I'm telling you, it still is. Just not as respectable. Now they are ordinary kothi khanas pretending to be the real thing."

Razaq stared at him in the mirror. He didn't understand everything the man said, but was he warning them? Were they being taken to a brothel? Razaq carefully tried his door but it was locked.

He felt Tahira's hand on his. "What is the matter?" she whispered.

"We have to get you out of here."

"Why? Whatever happens it will happen whether we are at Mr. Malik's house or this new place."

Razaq hated how her voice sounded so tired. "We could live on the street," he said, thinking of Zakim.

"It will be even worse. And Mr. Malik knows many people. They would find us."

"I know a place," he said stubbornly.

Tahira looked at him. He could see the sadness on her face as they drove under the streetlights. How would he and Zakim keep her safe at the scrap yard? As soon as the bear saw her, he would tell his landlord, and she'd be sold all over again. How long would Zakim be able to keep Moti safe? Why did men treat girls this way? Razaq had a trade now: he could be a malishia honorably if he worked for himself like Zakim did. Whenever a man said, "What else?" Razaq would be able to say, "Sorry, nothing else, just expert malish, janab." He gave a sad smile in the dark.

He heard the train and knew they were back in Rawalpindi where he'd rescued the buffalo at Farawa Chowk. He leaned forward and asked the driver, "Where is Qasai Gali?"

The driver tooted his horn, then said, "Behind Moti Bazaar. It is as big and busy as an ants' nest, so remember what I said. Don't get lost and don't talk to anyone you do not know. People steal good-looking kids like you."

Razaq scowled. It was a bit late for that advice.

Murad gave a grunt and the driver shut up. The car turned down a gali barely wide enough for it, lined with adjoining houses. Murad got out and Razaq saw a glint in his hand: he had a gun.

Murad looked up and down the gali before opening Razaq's door. He motioned with the gun for both of them to get out Razaq's side, then herded them toward a door. There was music coming from an upstairs window, and at ground level, there were windows where they saw women without scarves singing and dancing. Tahira pulled her own shawl tighter around herself. Razaq looked down the gali; it wasn't a hive of activity, but he could imagine stalls set up there in the daytime. A group of young men entered the lane, laughing together.

Murad pounded on the door. It opened immediately as if they had been expected. A girl, older than Tahira, stood there, her bold gaze taking in Murad and then Razaq. Her eyes widened. "Ji?"

Murad thrust Razaq and Tahira into the house, pushing the girl aside. A woman appeared. "Murad, put that gun away. Do you think you are a movie star?" Murad frowned. "So, these are Malik's little beauties."

The woman flowed closer as the girl shut the door. The woman was thin with a hooked nose and wore an orange shalwar qameez that barely covered her chest. Her glass bangles clinked and the sound reminded Razaq of his home. His sisters loved those glass bangles, especially red ones, but they broke so easily.

The woman—Mrs. Mumtaz, Razaq suspected—pulled off Tahira's shawl and peered at her. She took Razaq's chin in her hand and lifted his head to see his eyes. "Hmm. Malik spoke truly for once. We should put you to breeding. Fair green-eyed girls would make us a fortune."

Razaq scowled. How dare someone talk to him as if he were a ram!

Mrs. Mumtaz laughed, then gave Razaq a smack on his cheek with her open palm. Perhaps she meant it playfully, but it still hurt.

"Ow."

"Ow," she mimicked. "Is that all you can say, mountain wolf?"

He narrowed his eyes at her. Saleem had called him a wolf, too. His fingers clenched as he breathed in quickly, then he felt Tahira's hand on his arm. He slowly let the air out.

Mrs. Mumtaz watched them. "So, this is true also. Malik says you are a pair." She opened her eyes wide at Razaq but still he said nothing. Her face changed. "Even if you do have feelings for this one, you will bury them. She is not for you. And if I find you interfering with her or any of my girls without permission . . ." She grabbed Razaq in the front of his shalwar. He gasped in shock as she made a chopping motion with her other hand, then let him go. "And I can see that would be a big pity."

Her eyes flashed at him. "All you have to do is obey one rule." She paused as if telling a joke. "And that is to obey me. I am the naika, the madam. Understand?"

Tahira nodded. Razaq did, too. He could see Mrs. Mumtaz was capable of anything, maybe even of making Tahira's life hell if he didn't do what she wanted.

She walked around him, considering him. "You are the only boy I have working here. You are on probation only. Malik tells me you are a malishia. This is good. We have a room for you and also for you, little sweetie."

She turned to Tahira and Razaq stiffened as her long red fingernail traced a line down Tahira's cheek to the corner of her mouth. "This is where my knife will cut if you refuse a customer, or if you forget to give me any tips or gifts you receive. Do you understand?"

Razaq could see Tahira blinking, trying to keep the tears at bay.

"She is only twelve," he said. Even he could hear the challenge in his tone, and he sensed Murad take a step closer to him.

"So, the wolf speaks at last and not on his own behalf. How interesting. She is twelve, you say? Well, that is just how my customers like it." Mrs. Mumtaz stared into Razaq's eyes, daring him to say more, but he decided against it.

She waved Murad off then. "Tell Malik they will do fine."

As the girl shut the door behind him, Mrs. Mumtaz smiled again. "You both are my Eid-ul-Adha gift."

Her smiles were even worse than Mr. Malik's, Razaq thought. She looked like a jackal and was just as unpredictable.

She took them past the room where the girls were dancing to the tabla and harmonium. The musicians were playing a love song that reminded Razaq of Uncle Javaid's wedding. Men lounged against cushions watching the girls. None of the men wore suit coats or fine leather shoes, and they seemed to be having fun. Apart from the fact that men in the mountains didn't sit around and watch women dance, it looked innocent enough. The house was older, the rooms smaller, and the furniture not as fine as at the white house, but the place seemed warm and cozy in the low light.

Razaq was given a room facing the gali. Mrs. Mumtaz stayed in the hall as he entered. He turned at the sound of the door closing and a bolt shooting home. He raced to the door and pulled at it, but it wouldn't budge. He checked the window, but it had bars—there would be no getting out of that.

The room was small and filled mostly by the bed, but there was a wash bowl and a bucket of water, plus another bucket—no doubt the toilet, for there was a lota, a small plastic jug, beside it to wash his bottom if needed. Razaq sank onto the bed. It was a dump compared to his room in the white house but still a palace compared to Zakim's cardboard Rag Mahal.

In the morning, Razaq was standing at the window when his door was unbolted and the girl from the night before stood there with a tray. It held chai, a chapatti, and some leftover potato curry. So the food wasn't the same as the white house's either. Razaq sighed inwardly as the girl sidled in and dumped the tray on the bed. The chai spilled onto the tray.

"You are very handsome, Mr. Green Eyes," she said. "Like Hrithik Roshan." She smirked at his incomprehension. "The Bollywood actor—you see his latest movie?"

Razaq looked at her thin face and frowned. What sort of girl said something like that to a boy? She came closer and if Razaq could have taken a step backward, he would have.

"My name is Neelma, and I am Mrs. Mumtaz's niece."

Razaq felt a cold mist rise over him, as if a jinn had flown through the window. If Mrs. Mumtaz found her here she'd get her knife out, he was sure of it.

"You must leave my room." It came out as a croak.

She pouted. "I am not frightened of my aunt if that is what you are worried about. I do not work here; I live here. One day I will be the madam."

Razaq wasn't taking any chances, but he didn't want to offend the girl either. She had a petulant look, as if she could be spiteful when crossed. He'd seen that expression on a boy's face at the madrasah when Ardil had quoted all his verses correctly. On the way home, the boy had tripped Ardil, and he'd hurt his ankle.

Suddenly, the girl smiled. Razaq let out a breath he didn't realize he'd been holding.

"You are still new," she said. "There is time to get to know each other." Then she paused. "Today is a special day—Eid-ul-Adha— but you will not be celebrating since you are locked in here."

Razaq couldn't decide why she was pointing out the obvious: was she sorry about it or being mean? She left the room with a wink. He'd had no idea girls could be so forward.

"And," she put her head back in the room, "you empty that bucket in the latrine in the courtyard. When you are allowed out, that is. In the meantime, the jamadarni will do it each morning." She grinned, shut the door and shot the bolt across.

Razaq ate the curry using the chapatti to scoop it up as he always did; it was cold. So was the chai, but he drank it anyway. In the mountains, he had helped his father slaughter the goat for the sacrifice of Eid-ul-Adha to remember Ibrahim almost sacrificing his son Ismail, but God provided a ram in time. Last year, Razaq's mother had divided the meat for their neighbors, and he took some to Ardil's house. His mother made a delicious curry from the goat, and they

130

ate well for three whole days. His father had praised not only his wife's cooking but also Razaq for raising such tasty meat.

Razaq stood and paced the length of the room. He had never been locked in such a small space. Even though he couldn't get out of the white house, he could still walk down the hallway, sit in the dancing room, watch TV. Now he did feel like a wolf. A wolf in a cage would yearn for the mountains, the freedom to run and hunt. It would snarl and fight the bars at first, but eventually the futility would kill it as surely as a bullet would. The freedom of the mountains was so much a part of Razaq that he was frightened of what he would become without it.

Chapter 19

Each morning, the door opened and a woman in rags came in to take Razaq's latrine bucket. She must be the jamadarni, Razaq thought. He had never seen one before, but he'd heard that they swept the streets in cities and emptied commodes and garbage bins. He curled up tighter under the cotton-filled quilt like he used to when he was little. He would have done anything right then to see his mother come into the room, bend over him, and pull his ears to rouse him up to take the goats to a new field.

He woke later to find a tray of food on the floor by the bed, but he didn't bother to eat it. A cockroach crawled on the rim of the curry dish; orange oil congealed around the edges. Perhaps he could stay asleep forever. He closed his eyes.

A knock on the door woke him, but he ignored it. It came again. It would be that terrible girl. Then he remembered how she had barged in; she wouldn't knock. He heard his name called. It didn't sound like Neelma. He pulled back the quilt and padded to the door. He pulled on the knob and miraculously it opened.

Tahira stood there. "Razaq," she said, "you look dreadful."

He half-grinned. "Shukriya, kind princess."

Her face darkened. "Don't call me that."

He sobered. "I am sorry."

She touched his arm. "I knew you wouldn't like to be locked up. Mrs. Mumtaz did it because you're a boy, and she needs to be sure you will cooperate." She stumbled over "cooperate" and Razaq frowned. He could hear Mrs. Mumtaz's words in Tahira's mouth. "I told her if she let you out in the afternoons, you would do the right thing."

"I wish you hadn't done that." He imagined the begging Mrs. Mumtaz would have made her endure.

"But look at you—you are so dark and sad. You have lost your light, like you've been under a rock all week."

Razaq remembered Zakim saying he had light in his eyes. "Has it truly been a week?" he asked.

"Almost."

"Does Mrs. Mumtaz know you are here?"

She nodded. "You can't have breakfast with the girls, but you can sit in the courtyard later on, or go on the roof if the girls go outside."

Razaq felt a lifting sensation inside him. "You are a true friend, Tahira." It made her smile. "Have you . . . have you started work yet?"

The smile faded. "I had to start dancing last night. I danced in the room with the women and girls, and then I danced for a man in my room. After that," she said softly, "another came."

"I am sorry," Razaq said. "I wish I could do something."

Her eyes were large. "I pray to Yesu and I feel less." Then she said, "I never dreamed this. I wanted to go to high school. There is a boarding school for Christian girls in the mountains. My friend Hadassah went—an Angrez paid for her fees. That would have happened for me, too, for I gained the same marks as Hadassah. Then I would become a teacher. After that . . ." Her voice trailed off, but Razaq knew what should have come after: a shadi, a wedding. "None of that will happen now," she whispered.

Razaq didn't trust himself to say anything. The anger that men like Mr. Malik could take everything away from girls like Tahira rose up behind his eyes and consumed him. He could have punched the wall, but he didn't want to frighten her.

Instead he said, "I was meant to be married in three years."

She frowned at him. "Aren't you too young?"

He glanced up the corridor before he said, "Boys marry young in the mountains, at seventeen even. I am older than Mr. Malik thinks. I just didn't tell him. I got away with it because I am not tall."

"You are growing," she said. "You are taller than when you first came to Mr. Malik's house." Then she added thoughtfully, "All I can hope for is to become a tawaif, a high-class prostitute, with only one man looking after me. It is a kind of shadi." She made a sad sound. "The only way out of this life now would be to marry, but who will marry a girl like me?"

Razaq wanted to say that he would like to, but would it change everything if he told her? Now she knew he was older than she was, she might keep away from him, and they both needed this friendship.

"What was your dream?" she asked.

He grinned. "Look after the land we worked and build up a herd of sheep from our ram Peepu that every man in the mountains would want for his own herd. But the earthquake changed all that."

"I must go," she said suddenly, as if she heard a noise. "I will try to see you if you come to the courtyard."

Razaq didn't have a chance to check out the courtyard because Mrs. Mumtaz visited him next.

"I didn't think you would like to be locked in, but that is what will happen if I have any tuklief from you." She put a folded shalwar qameez and a towel on the bed. "Wash and put this on. I see you have your bottles of oil. Good. A customer will come shortly. At first there will only be a few customers until it becomes known we have a malishia." She narrowed her eyes at him. "Do a good job and make me happy."

Razaq thought it was a good time to ask about his pay. "Will you be putting aside money for me each time?"

"God, you mountain people think you own the world, don't you?"

"With respect, bibi, Mr. Malik put aside money for me each time a customer came. Do you have it?"

She stared at him so long that Razaq couldn't tell whether he'd offended her or if she would start laughing. Finally, she said in a strangely controlled voice, "Is that what he told you?"

"Ji."

"He didn't give me your little bank account, so you had better start afresh. Teik hai, I can put aside money for you, but half of what you earn has to go to Malik, and half to me for looking after you and housing you. I can put away twenty rupees each time."

"But the customer pays so much more, and I am the one doing the work."

She put a hand on the door and looked back at him. "But you do not work for yourself, do you? Malishia work is a very profitable business, and this is the first I've heard of one working for someone else."

"I could work for myself," Razaq said.

"I'm sure you could, but Malik needs his lakh first. That will take twice as long since you are working here."

She smiled, showing her jackal fangs, then swung out of the room as though she was as young as Neelma. Razaq listened carefully, but there was no sound of a bolt drawn across. It was amazing how good that felt: he could open the door if he wanted.

Instead, he washed himself and combed his hair, put on the clean suit of clothes. It was embroidered with light pink thread and had a neck shaped like a valley. His father always wore qameezes with buttons and collars, and so had he. Then his door opened and a good-looking young man ushered in an older man. The younger man saluted Razaq before he closed the door again.

The customer stood by the door. "I've never had a massage before," he said, "but I have hurt my shoulder. Could you ease it?"

Razaq was lost for words for a moment. "You want an upper back massage?" he finally said.

The man nodded.

"I shall try. Please, take off your qameez and lie here." Razaq spread the towel on the bed.

The man winced as he took off his shirt and lay down. As Razaq worked on the man's shoulder, he felt his first twinge of self-respect since he had entered Mr. Malik's house. He would like to be able to make people feel better in this way. His mother had a talent with herbs yet Razaq had never paid attention. He thought it was women's business, for his mother was called upon if a friend was giving birth.

He massaged the rest of the man's back as well—he was sure it would all be connected. The man groaned, but he didn't sound displeased.

When it was finished and the man put on his shirt, he smiled. "It feels much better. Thank you, what is your good name?"

"Razaq."

He felt a prickling behind his eyes; that was the way his father asked the name of a man. None of his customers had ever thanked him like that either, and there had been no "whatever." If only all his customers could be like this one.

"If I get any more pain I shall return," the man said.

When the door opened, Razaq saw the young man sitting on the floor in the hallway. He stood up to escort the customer outside.

"Who are you?" Razaq asked when the young man returned.

"I am Bilal and I am your madadgar, your helper." He grinned. "Actually, now that men are coming into the house in the afternoons to see you, I have to provide security."

Razaq's mouth dropped open. "Truly?"

Bilal was a heavy young man. Even though his voice sounded like a boy's, Razaq could imagine him "providing security" like Murad did, but he was nicer than Murad.

"Mrs. M doesn't want any trouble," Bilal said. "Besides, it beats sitting around. I am here in the evenings as well to watch that no one hurts the girls. The customers need to know there is a man in the house." He grimaced.

Razaq was amazed he hadn't known there was another male here. Hadn't Mrs. Mumtaz said Razaq was the only boy? Why hadn't she mentioned Bilal?

"Don't you find it difficult living here with the girls?" he asked.

A shadow passed quickly over Bilal's face. "I manage." Then he said, "Come, I will show you something."

He took Razaq down the corridor and out a door. The brightness made Razaq squint his eyes.

"We have to go behind this screen so you don't see the girls in the courtyard," Bilal said.

Razaq wondered why Bilal didn't include himself in that rule. He led Razaq up two flights of steps until they stood on the flat concrete roof. Razaq gasped. It was like being given a gift. A breeze blew his hair. It was cold, and he hadn't brought his vest, but he didn't care. He lifted his arms wide, threw back his head, and laughed at the sky. He could hear the tabla playing and danced, then realized it was Bilal clapping. He stood still and looked out over the gali with its street stalls and people milling about. Between buildings he could see a kite flying. He kept turning until he saw everything: the minarets, the clouds, hills in the distance. He sighed.

Bilal pointed out landmarks. "There's Qila Fort. Moti Bazaar. The Christian girls' college." He watched Razaq. "I thought you would like it up here. You look like someone used to being outside. I used to bring your food when you wouldn't get out of bed."

"Neelma brought it the first time."

"That fox, she tricked me to let her do it that morning because it was Eid, but I'm not getting into trouble for her."

"Shukriya." Razaq squinted at the northern horizon. "I come from the mountains, but they are so far away I cannot see them."

Bilal grunted.

"What about you?" Razaq asked. "How did you come here?"

"I was the same age as you. Came to the city for work. Slept in the bus adda, sold shoelaces to travelers. I made enough to buy food in the evening. Then a driver offered me a job cleaning his bus. Twenty rupees a day. It sounded like a fortune."

Razaq thought of Saleem's boy and tried to keep the pity from his face. How many did it happen to? "And how did you get here?"

"My bus driver had an accident. He didn't return and I ran. I was more careful after that, but not careful enough. I took a job with the wrong man and now I am here." He sighed. "At least this place is better than a low-class kothi khana in the city—they are run by men, and they beat you. And you get ten, twelve customers all day and night, and they don't want dancing or massages, they just give you diseases." He paused and took out a pouch with cigarette papers and tobacco in it. "Here I have a place to sleep, food, a job."

But no life, Razaq thought, *no future*. He wanted to carry on his father's line, have descendants who would honor his father's name, and he wanted to do that with Tahira. But how could he now? He saw the years stretch out before him—a gray wasteland.

"I had dreams," Bilal said, a cigarette in the corner of his mouth. "Want one? It will make you feel better."

He held out the pouch. Razaq declined with his hand.

"Maybe the movies," Bilal went on. "Be an actor. I would be famous, have money to help kids like me, but it was stupid."

"It happens to some," Razaq said.

"Only a few. But they might still be slaves." He blew smoke into the air.

Razaq wrapped his arms around his knees. "I want to be free," he murmured.

Bilal narrowed his eyes at him. "Don't let Mrs. M hear you say that. She thinks she's a rani ruling over her little kingdom, and she can't be crossed. If she orders me to beat you, I will have to do it." He stared at Razaq a moment too long, and Razaq looked away. "Besides, there is no way to get free unless a miracle happens and someone buys you out. Or you just wait until you have paid your debt."

"I will be old by then," Razaq said.

How long before he could pay off the lakh? Could he even trust Mr. Malik and Mrs. Mumtaz? Was anything written down? How much had he lost already by Mr. Malik not giving him what he had earned in the white house? By the look on Mrs. Mumtaz's face, none of it had been true anyway, and would she put money aside for him even though she had said she would? He'd never be sure of them, never free. Maybe he should just try to run. Then he thought of Tahira. How could he leave her alone?

"You are a beautiful boy," Bilal said.

Razaq glanced at him sharply but saw no guile in his stare.

"Be careful," he continued. "Some people cannot understand beauty, and what they don't understand they destroy."

There was such bitterness in Bilal's tone that Razaq didn't feel he could ask what he meant.

Chapter 20

Javaid had used his cell phone to call all the places he had found on the Web—organizations that helped find missing children and nongovernment agencies working against trafficking. He had even found some centers for street children set up by Western aid agencies. No one had seen Razaq, but he was now listed in their databases. All Javaid could do was keep looking. He had to believe Razaq was still in the city.

Amina gently asked him to consider whether he should give up the search. "I hardly see you anymore," she said. "And Sakina misses you."

Javaid sighed. Some nights he came home so late after work Sakina was already asleep, and the nights he visited Amina's bed, he fell asleep too soon in her arms.

"What if he only comes onto the street at night?" he said.

Amina stared at him sadly. "You still have Sakina. Do not neglect her."

Javaid sat on the bed and pulled Amina to sit beside him. "There is something I need to tell you." He blew out an audible breath. "When I was a boy, a teacher in the madrasah did something indecent to me." Amina's eyes widened. "Yes, it is why I found it difficult when we were first married."

"I wondered," she whispered.

"I always felt weak for not putting up a fight. Nadeem said I should put a stop to it. He would have, I suppose." Javaid looked down at his hands. "Anyway, I left the mountains as soon as I could. I felt I wasn't a mountain man like Nadeem. He thought I was a coward for living in the city." He looked at Amina. "So please understand, I have to find Razaq—not just for me or for Nadeem, but for Razaq, to save him from what happened to me."

Amina put a hand on either side of his face. "I do not think you are a coward. What happened to you isn't who you are."

Javaid smiled sadly. "I know that now, but I didn't know it when I needed to."

❋

Javaid took to leaving earlier in the mornings. He spent the time asking in shops on the way to work. He even tried the local carpet factories on his day off.

"Your nephew would be too old for this kind of intricate work," said the last factory manager he saw.

He showed Javaid into the shed. Young boys not much older than Sakina sat cross-legged at a loom, cutting and tying knots. Their hands blurred, they moved so fast. A man stood nearby holding a pattern sheet.

"This is not a forced labor place, you understand," the man said quickly when he saw Javaid's face. "Ji, these boys are only six or so, but their fingers make the best knots. Also they are earning for their families. We let them play soccer in the afternoons and teach them some letters and numbers." He waggled his head. "It is a good arrangement."

None of the boys looked up, so Javaid couldn't tell if they were ill treated.

The manager watched him. "If your nephew is on the streets, janab, he will be working in the scrap yards."

Chapter 21

Mrs. Mumtaz was very pleased with Razaq. She ordered Bilal to buy pastries from the bakery for his lunch. "I am getting good reports about you, mountain wolf. You keep this up and you will eat very well indeed."

Most of the time, the customers only wanted ordinary massages, and Razaq didn't have to say "whatever you want." More men were coming to the house. Many would have a massage in the late afternoon and then watch the girls dance in the evening. Razaq hoped that if any of the men he massaged danced with Tahira later, he had put them in a gentle mood.

He had almost forgotten how "whatever" felt when a middle-aged customer was shown into his room. The man stood transfixed, staring at Razaq's eyes and brown hair flopping onto his forehead. "What do you do?" he said.

Razaq's heart dipped. "Massages, janab." He caught the inside of his cheek between his teeth, hoping that was the end of it, hoping his tone sounded as if that was all he did.

"And what else?" the man asked softly.

Razaq hesitated. If he refused, maybe the man would just leave. But maybe he would complain to Mrs. Mumtaz, and maybe she would cut Tahira's face because Razaq had refused a customer.

"Whatever you want." Razaq said the hated words, and the man pulled off his qameez and untied his shalwar.

"Then massage me everywhere until I feel I can fly." He grabbed Razaq's wrist. "And I mean everywhere, boy."

When Sunni had come back that morning in the white house, he had taught Razaq how to make customers feel as if they could conquer the world. The man moaned. "You do this better than the girls," he said. It struck horror into Razaq's heart. What had he become?

Mrs. Mumtaz was even more pleased. "I am told you have a talent." Her kohl-colored eyes flashed at him with interest. "Tonight you can dance with the girls."

By six o'clock, the Mirasi, the musicians, had arrived with their tabla and harmonium. Razaq could hear their music when Mrs. Mumtaz came to his room with an outfit.

"I want you to wear this," she said.

Razaq saw the bright green and blue fabric. It sparkled. "What is it?"

"You'll find out. I'll expect you in a few minutes."

Razaq unfolded the clothes and dropped them on the floor as if they were aflame. The shalwar had splits down the sides, and the top wasn't a shirt but a short silk vest. All his middle would show. He stepped back as far as he could from the clothes. She was trying to turn him into a lakhtai, a dancer boy. Danyal had worn something like this in the white house, but he was only young.

He heard Mrs. Mumtaz calling him. He sighed and picked up the shalwar and pulled it on. It was tight and his backside stuck out. He was sure his legs and maybe part of his buttock would be seen when he danced.

His door flew open. "What are you doing?" It was Mrs. Mumtaz. When she saw him, she smiled. "So, now we have a true mountain prince. We should call you Akbar, the Great."

She opened a kohl box in her hand and lined his eyes with the black powder. Razaq was miserable. If his father saw him like this, he'd kill him. He certainly wouldn't recognize him. Razaq didn't recognize himself.

"A jao, come." Mrs. Mumtaz motioned quickly with her hand. "Let me show off my prize. Just act normally, you'll soon get used to playing a crowd."

She swept him into the music room. There were customers arriving and others already sitting on cushions around the walls. Hookah pipes stood in the corners. A few girls were dancing. Tahira was one of them. When she twirled, she saw Razaq. He was not surprised by the horrified look on her face.

"Dance!" Mrs. Mumtaz hissed at him. She smiled at the men in the room.

The men began clapping. Razaq danced a mixture of mountain folk dance and the moves Pretty had taught him in Mr. Malik's house. "Charming," one man said, and Mrs. Mumtaz's smile grew wider, even though Razaq knew his dancing was halfhearted.

He tried to edge closer to Tahira, to explain. Would she want anything to do with him now? Then he saw Neelma in the hallway, watching him with the stillness of a fox on her face, and he thought better of putting Tahira in danger.

When a man asked Razaq if he could visit his room, Tahira was still dancing. Razaq's only consolation was that he may have saved her a customer.

The nights Razaq danced, he had to do more "whatevers." When his mind and body complained, he thought of poor Tahira having to do this every night. He tried to think of the mountains instead of what he was doing: how Machay Sar looked with snow covering its peak. How the leopards ran free up there, although he had only ever seen one. He was eleven, it had been Eid-ul-Fitr the week before and his father had given him the gun. They trekked together to the foothills of the highest mountain and found the huge tracks.

"A young leopard," his father said, "only a few years old."

Then Razaq caught a glimpse of it balanced on a rock, looking back at them. "There it is." He lifted his rifle. "Should we take it, Abu ji? The fur looks warm."

His father pushed the gun barrel down. "Many would, beta, but leopard killing must stop. The leopard is too beautiful to take for ourselves. It needs to run free. If one gives itself to us, then we can have its pelt for the winter."

Razaq understood: if the leopard should die of natural causes and they found its body, then the pelt would be theirs. That day, they hunted a goral, a goat antelope. It was Razaq's first kill.

�֍

Bilal came to Razaq's door one day before lunch. Razaq had just woken up. "Get up," Bilal said. "Mrs. M has allowed you to come to the bazaar with me." He grinned. "She must be very pleased with you." Then his grin disappeared. "But if you run off, I will find you and kill you for she will never trust me again."

He raised his eyebrows and Razaq inclined his head. As he got out of bed, Bilal cuffed him playfully over the head. "We will have chai before the jobs Mrs. M has given me to do. Then you can help carry everything. You have to be back before your customers come in the afternoon."

Razaq used the bucket, then washed his face, smoothed down his hair. How long was it since he had been outside, other than on the roof? Was it months? He had lost count.

"A jao." Bilal held the door open.

As they went into the hallway and headed outside, Razaq caught sight of Neelma watching them from the courtyard where the kitchen was. As they walked onto the gali, Razaq said, "Mrs. Mumtaz knows we are going?"

"Ji, why are you worried?"

"I saw Neelma watching us."

Bilal glanced at Razaq. "You need to be careful. She is throwing her heart at you."

"Why not you? You are older, and you are handsome."

A dark look came over Bilal's face. "She will have no happiness from me."

Razaq grinned at him. "Why not? Has Mrs. Mumtaz forbidden you also?"

"I have been cut."

Razaq stood still. *Cut?* He tried to keep his eyes from Bilal's shalwar, but all he could think of was Mrs. Mumtaz grabbing him the first night he came. Bilal stopped for him to catch up, but Razaq couldn't ask what he wanted. Bilal took him to a teashop and they sat while the chai came.

"What did you mean?" Razaq finally asked.

"Just what I said. Do not upset Mrs. M or you may find out for yourself sooner or later."

"Why did she do it?"

Bilal pursed his lips. "I just got too old. I didn't like being here—she thought I would give her trouble."

Razaq's breath caught in his throat. "How old were you?"

"Thirteen. When my mustache began growing, five years ago. She thought I'd be more useful this way. Some customers even like it."

Razaq tried not to stare, but he felt the fear, could feel the knife as if it had happened to him. He would have to make sure that Mrs. Mumtaz didn't find out how old he was. He thought of the rams his father had kept for breeding, and the few that he had castrated to keep for meat. That was all he and Bilal were to Mrs. Mumtaz: lumps of meat.

Being in the bazaar, almost free, no longer held any thrill. Bilal was giving him a warning, he knew. They went to numerous shops. Bilal had a list; each shopkeeper took it and loaded household items into plastic bags for the boys to carry. Razaq suspected that Bilal couldn't read. His own reading was sketchy, but he could make out most things if given time. He could see that Bilal had no option but to keep living this life that had been given him—not by his parents or by God, but by Mrs. Mumtaz. Anger rose inside him at the thought. What right did adults like her have to change children's lives from their God-given path?

Razaq found the anger gave him a feeling he had forgotten: of being alive, still himself. Maybe the imagined freedom of being in the gali and bazaar had helped after all.

When they returned, he went up on the roof, hoping Tahira had noticed him go. He sat and stared out over the part of the city that he could see—Qila Fort on the northern side of the bazaars—and heard the squeals from girls playing a game in the school. Somewhere nearby was Moti Bazaar where his uncle worked. Razaq wiped a hand over his eyes. What was the use of thinking of his uncle? He wouldn't want to know his nephew now. He was a bucket that had been left outside in the rain—tarnished, with holes in it; a bucket his mother would have thrown away.

"Razaq?"

He started and stood. He hadn't dared hope, but it was Tahira. His smile disappeared when he saw the purple shadow under her eyes. "What is this?" He stretched out a hand to touch it gently.

"A customer saw my cross, and he hit me."

Razaq turned away so she wouldn't see his anger. His mother had always told him to take his anger away from her eyes.

"Razaq?"

He heard the hurt in her voice and faced her. "I am sorry," he said, "but I could kill anyone who harms you."

She smiled sadly. "My brother used to say that, too."

"This is all so wrong," he muttered. Tahira shouldn't be hit by men. He shouldn't be in fear of losing his manhood. He saw the concern on her face and calmed himself. "What is your cross?"

She pulled out a necklace. It was made of gold and looked like a four-pointed star. "An Angrez lady gave it to my mother."

Razaq opened the buttons on his qameez and showed her the silver tarveez his father always wore. "Is it like this for you? It has verses of the Quran in it to keep me safe."

Tahira said softly, "My cross is to remember who I am."

He thought her eyes looked dazed today. "Is something the matter?" he asked.

"It is Ismat, one of the girls. She was sold to pay off a debt, but her parents never thought she would end up in a chakla like this. She is sadder lately. We are asked to do such bad things. Sometimes evil men come."

Razaq clenched his fingers; he hated the thought of Tahira dancing with someone else. "Aren't they all evil?"

She seemed to make an effort to focus on him. "Not all. Last night a man came to dance with me, but he didn't dance at all. He talked."

"He paid for that?"

She nodded. "His wife died. He wanted me to hold him." She sighed. "But still I shouldn't be holding strange men, even if they don't dance."

"It will be all right," he said. "I will think of something to help us escape." He wondered if he believed it himself.

She stared at him; her eyes were losing focus again. "No one can help. Mrs. Mumtaz doesn't care about us. There is only one good thing about Mrs. Mumtaz."

Razaq raised an eyebrow. This would be interesting.

"She lets me read my Injil, my holy book. If I went out of my village, I was not respected because I wasn't Muslim. But she doesn't care what I believe." Tahira glanced at him. "She doesn't think I can truly read my Injil, but she hasn't taken it away."

Razaq couldn't read the Quran for it was in Arabic. Only the maulvi could read it. So, Tahira's Injil must be written in Urdu. How could that be?

"It is my only bright spot in the day," she added.

And you are my bright spot, Razaq thought.

"Tahira!" Neelma's voice called from the courtyard.

They both stared at each other. Razaq could see the fear flowering in Tahira's eyes. Were his any different?

"I am not allowed on the roof," she whispered.

"Then I will go first and talk to her while you come down."

She watched him as he walked down the steps. He smiled at her the whole way, but it was an effort to act as though they weren't in danger.

Inside the hallway, he encountered Neelma. "Have you seen Tahira?" she said. "She has work to do."

He tried to shrug casually. "Maybe she is in the latrine."

She looked up at him. With a pang, he realized he was growing. Hadn't she been closer to his height that first morning?

"She is just a child," Neelma said. "I am a woman."

If Razaq wasn't covering for Tahira he would have run to his room. Instead, he forced himself to stand there.

"Your aunt has forbidden me to touch you," he said.

"I do not believe you."

"It is true." Razaq put a sad look on his face.

Neelma sidled closer. "We don't have to do what she says."

Razaq thought of Bilal and closed his eyes. He certainly did have to do what Mrs. Mumtaz said.

Neelma must have taken his silence for agreement for she reached up and planted a kiss on his mouth. His eyes flew open and he backed away. Neelma was smiling. Above her head, he could see Tahira opening the latrine door.

"I am sorry," he said, "I must go. I have customers soon."

Neelma's smile faded, but she didn't look unhappy. She turned toward the courtyard. "Tahira! Are you in there? Hurry up, you lazy child."

She twisted to look back at Razaq with such a smug smile that it made dread rise in him like a storm.

Chapter 22

Javaid had visited several scrap yards. Some even had tiny children working in them. Today, he decided to try closer to Moti Bazaar. It was the last place where he had heard news of Razaq, and his father had always told him and Nadeem to stay close to where you first became lost in the forest so it was easier to be found. Surely, Razaq had been told the same advice? Javaid was seeing the city more and more as a jungle with wild animals and harsh, dangerous conditions. He knew it was a long shot for Razaq to be at a scrap heap so close to the bazaar because he hadn't made contact, but Amina was right. The search had become an obsession now. He couldn't give up.

He found the gateway in. A truck had just backed up and dumped a pile of scrap; it rolled down near his shoes. He wished he wore a turban and could use it to cover his nose: the stench was putrid. There were tiny children scouring the new material. They looked like flies clustered on a festering wound. Javaid's thoughts were grim. So this was how the government got the recycling done.

He approached a few of the children, but they scattered like a brood of chickens. They were frightened of him. He saw a tall, heavy boy and picked his way carefully over to him.

"Assalamu alaikum," Javaid said.

The boy didn't give the return greeting, just glared at him. He only had one eye; a scar ran down through his empty socket and ended under his shirt somewhere. Javaid winced internally. That would have been nasty. So it was dangerous in the scrap yard, too.

"What do you want here?" The boy was belligerent.

"I am looking for someone."

The boy's expression seemed to say, So?

Javaid sighed. "Have you seen a mountain boy working here?"

"I"ve seen plenty. You want to kill one?"

He looked eager suddenly, and Javaid backed away. He had never seen this side of the city. He wondered where the boy slept.

He saw more children in the distance and thought he would try once more, but they all dispersed as he approached. One moment his head was down watching where he put his feet amongst the muck, and the next the children were gone as if they had been vaporized. He felt stupid. Nothing he had done all these months had worked. He should take notice of his wife and stop looking.

He did the only thing he could think of: he shouted, "Razaq! Razaq! Are you here?" as he turned a full circle. When he reached its end, a small girl was standing not far from him. He took a step forward, but she made to run so he stopped.

"Have you seen Razaq?" he said.

"Why do you want him?"

An older boy ran up and shooed her away, then he stood in her place staring at Javaid. "Who are you?" he finally asked.

"Javaid Khan. I have a nephew, Abdur-Razaq. I need to find him."

"Why?"

Javaid regarded him. What happened to these children to make them so suspicious? "He is my family." His voice cracked. "I want to take him home."

The boy slowly walked closer. He wore a dirty white cap and his skin was fairer than most Pakistanis. A hooked nose. He looked Afghan. Was this where the refugee children ended up? Javaid felt guilt at having a comfortable life while this child had to work on a dung heap.

"Do you have a boss I can ask about my nephew?" he said, trying not to let his distress show.

The boy lifted his chin. "I answer to no one. You can ask me what you want to know."

Javaid almost smiled. The boy had spirit. "Razaq—have you seen him?"

The boy's gaze never wavered from Javaid, but he hesitated as if deciding what to say. "There was a boy named Razaq here. He was very brave." The boy's eyes glistened, and Javaid looked away, suddenly afraid of what he might hear. "I would do anything to help him," the boy continued.

Javaid glanced back at him quickly. "He is here?"

The boy shook his head. "He went to find his Uncle Javaid. He said he would return."

"I have been searching for him also."

"So I heard," the boy said.

Javaid wondered what he meant. He felt uncomfortable under the boy's piercing gaze.

155

"Do you know where he is?" he asked. "Could you show me?"

The boy's eyes clouded a moment then resumed their stare. "Inshallah, God willing."

Javaid felt a lightening inside; it was the first ray of hope since that dreadful day of the earthquake.

He closed his eyes and whispered, "Alhamdulillah, thanks be to God."

Chapter 23

The next time Razaq went to the bazaar, he was allowed to go alone for Bilal was busy. He stopped at the pastry shop and asked for Mrs. Mumtaz's order. A police officer was standing behind him. As the bag was given to Razaq, the man said, "You are from the kothi khana, are you not?"

Razaq didn't answer. How could the man know unless he recognized Mrs. Mumtaz's name?

"We'll get you criminals," the man said.

Razaq jumped out of his way. Was it a warning or just bullying? Why didn't the policeman arrest him? If he did, Razaq could say he was being forced to stay there.

Mrs. Mumtaz was in the courtyard when he took the supplies to the kitchen. He decided not to mention the incident; he didn't want his little trips to the bazaar stopped—it was the only bit of normal life he had.

She narrowed her eyes at him. "Why were you so long?"

He didn't think he had been.

"Not doing anything you shouldn't, I hope."

Razaq couldn't think of anything she could mean and shook his head.

She took the bag of pastries from him, then frowned as she looked at him. She touched his lip. "What is this?"

Razaq didn't know; he didn't have a mirror.

She grabbed him by the ear and dragged him into a room. It had a mirror on the wall. "Look." She pushed his face toward it. He saw a pale-faced boy with light eyes staring out at him. He looked frightened. "Here." She pointed to his upper lip. He saw dark hairs there. He touched them; they felt soft as they always had. He hadn't realized they had a color.

"Undo your shalwar."

He opened his mouth in protest. "No."

She pursed her lips, and he untied the narda. She glanced at him and swore under her breath, as if the new hair on his body was his fault. "Do it up," she said.

A renewed dread descended on him. Bilal had said he had been cut when his mustache started. A glance at Mrs. Mumtaz didn't give him any clues about what would happen. She stood staring at him; he knew she was thinking hard.

"Chello, go to your room." The words whipped from her and he hurried out into the courtyard.

What would she do? Would praying help?

When he reached his room, he washed himself and stood on the mat. He had been taught that prayer was to adore God and not to ask for personal needs, but this was urgent. Would God listen, as Tahira believed?

Afterward, Razaq lay on the bed. The opening of the door startled him and he sat up. Bilal edged in with a tray and shut the door.

"So," he said, "you are to have a shave."

He lifted up an instrument. It looked like a shaving knife. Razaq had never seen his father shave, but once when Uncle Javaid came, Razaq saw him outside shaving the hair off his chin and cheeks. It had looked like he was scraping it off with a knife. His father had quarreled with his uncle after that, saying he'd lost his way of life.

Bilal spread some lather on Razaq's upper lip.

"Can't I do it?" Razaq said.

"Nay. Mrs. M's orders. You are not to touch the knife."

Razaq scowled at Bilal as he scraped off the hairs.

"That's done. Now untie your shalwar and lie down."

"Excuse me?" It came out as a squeak. Bilal seemed friendly enough, but Razaq knew he would do whatever Mrs. Mumtaz asked him to.

Bilal nodded at him and Razaq knew he wouldn't get out of it. He fumbled with the narda. "What are you going to do?" Could that shaver cut skin?

Bilal lifted up the lather stick. "Be thankful. Apparently, Mrs. M thinks you're worth keeping intact." He grinned. "Those green eyes and ghostly skin have saved you this time."

Razaq didn't like the emphasis on "this time."

"I think she is wanting a green-eyed grand-niece," Bilal added. "Good for business." He chuckled.

Razaq struggled to sit up.

"Keep still, you idiot, or you will be cut after all."

"I will never—can they make you do something like that?"

Bilal glanced up. "What haven't you been made to do?"

It was true. Ever since he met Ikram, things had happened to him that other people had ordered: Ikram, Kazim, Mr. Malik, and Mrs. Mumtaz. And now Mrs. Mumtaz wanted to keep him a boy forever, whichever way she could. How long would shaving keep him a boy? He was growing taller, too.

He wondered how Bilal felt seeing him get the second chance he was never offered.

It was not a good week for Razaq. That night, a customer came for a massage. The man stood inside the door, and a strange look came over his face when he focused on Razaq.

"Massage, janab?" Razaq prompted.

"Do you do more than massages?"

Razaq licked his top lip. "I give you whatever you want." He would never get used to that "whatever."

"I will give you something you will never forget." The man whisked a stick out of his shalwar. It looked like a policeman's baton. How did that get past Bilal? "If those lazy police don't do their job, I'll get rid of you criminals myself."

Before Razaq had the presence of mind to call for Bilal, the man threw him onto the bed. The force of it knocked the breath out of him, then came a burning pain on his head. Razaq screamed, but it only made the man more enraged. He kept beating Razaq with the stick, all the time shouting what vermin he was. Razaq tried to protect himself with his legs, his arms, even to distract the man, to talk, but the man didn't hear him. With growing horror, Razaq realized the man couldn't stop. He heard a crack and thought he would pass out with the pain, when Bilal burst in.

"Bas! Stop!" Bilal punched the man in the face, then wrestled the stick from him, pulled his arms behind him, and marched him toward the doorway. The man spat on Razaq as Bilal pushed him past.

After the outside door slammed, Bilal was back. "Are you okay? I am sorry I was late. Neelma was on the door, and she wouldn't have searched him."

He brought over the bucket of clean water. "Let me see the damage. Mrs. M will not be happy about your face."

Bilal fell silent as he undid Razaq's buttons and wiped the blood away. But some bleeding couldn't be stopped. He muttered and went out the door. Razaq had no energy to cover himself. From his head to his backside he felt he was on fire. He was barely conscious of Mrs. Mumtaz in the room, of Bilal arguing for the doctor.

"He needs the hospital, a proper doctor, not a kacha hakim. Please, I beg you, look at him."

The arguing went on in the courtyard, and Razaq tried to think of the cool forest on the ridge of the mountains, how he and Ardil used to track jackals up there near the old Angrez fort. Climbing down was like free falling from the walls of a building, but they both managed it without breaking any bones. Did Ardil ever get beaten? He had become so quiet after the khan's friend took him to his house, never said anything about his life there. Razaq had had no idea. Now he knew too much about the world, too much of what men could do.

When he came to, there was a man sitting on his bed. Bilal was behind him, watching. "He needs stitches," the man said. "I will give him opium for the pain."

So Mrs. Mumtaz had won: no hospital, only a healer who would be paid not to tell. If Razaq went to a hospital, he could tell the doctor what was happening here. Would they believe him?

Razaq clenched his teeth throughout the stitching of his head, but when Bilal and the hakim turned him over for more stitches, a jagged red color shot through his head, pulsating as if he could see it flashing on the wall. He screamed as he blacked out.

Razaq woke. At first he didn't remember, then he moved to get up and sank back with a groan. His head felt like the cotton his quilt was stuffed with. There was a bandage around his chest. How long had he been asleep? He had to get to the latrine. He sat up and clutched the bed, waiting for his head to stop swinging like a monkey through the trees. He pushed himself up to his feet, but his legs folded, and he fell. Maybe he could crawl to the bucket. He was not going to disgrace himself on the floor of his room like an animal in a cage. He dragged himself to the bucket and managed a crouch. He gasped with the pain, but at least he could still pee like a man.

Then he vomited. The pain racked his ribs and made him cry out. He sat on the floor, then thought better of that as well. Was there anywhere he didn't hurt? He crawled back to the bed and rested his head on the quilt. He didn't think his arms were strong enough to pull himself up fully.

When he woke again, he was lying on the bed and Bilal was putting a fresh shalwar on him. Razaq stared up at the ceiling. "This is the worst beating I've had," he said.

Bilal sat beside him. "It is the worst I have seen also. I have asked Mrs. M to give you a chutti, some time off from work."

Razaq tried to grin, but that hurt, too. "I can't massage like this."

"This is what I told her, but she said you were good for business. The sooner you are up, the better. She has given you until the stitches come out."

"When is that?"

"Ten days."

"I feel as if I will never get out of this room."

"You will heal, the hakim said. You are young."

But Razaq knew that in the places that mattered he would never heal.

He gazed at Bilal. "I feel old today. My grandfather was so frail he had to be held up to pee. Like me." He paused.

"That man said I was a criminal. Was he some sort of policeman?"

Bilal shook his head and made a face. "Just a crazy man." Then he leaned forward. "Razaq, what happened to you was wrong."

"Everything that has happened to me is wrong," Razaq murmured.

"The police say we are criminals, but it isn't our choice," Bilal said. "And they still take their pleasure before they arrest us. Hypocritical pigs."

Razaq wondered what had caused that outburst. Then he said, "Bilal, thank you. He couldn't stop—he would have killed me."

Chapter 24

It was a week before Razaq could walk without it hurting too much or crouch over the latrine bucket without excruciating pain. Everything seemed to hurt, but at least it wasn't that jagged red pain he had felt before he passed out. Bilal said it would be a month before he could sneeze or laugh. He had broken ribs before, too. Razaq didn't think he would ever laugh again. When had he last laughed? On the roof the first time Bilal took him up there? A few times with Tahira? Maybe he could force a smile to make her happy.

Before the ten days were up, Mrs. Mumtaz pushed him to the outside door. "Bilal is busy so you can get my pastries from the bakery. I see you won't be running away today." She watched him walking gingerly past her.

Outside on the gali, he should have enjoyed the breeze, the feeling of that small room rolling from him, but his mind was dull. He no longer thought of how he could get himself and Tahira out of Mrs. Mumtaz's house. He had no interesting thoughts at all. He was a different boy from the one who had charged into traffic he had never before encountered to rescue a buffalo. He winced as his foot bumped against a stone and jarred his leg. Why did his head feel like a wall built of stone and mud? He would give anything to be running wild in the terraced fields on the slopes of the mountain near his home with Ardil. In September, the grass was so thick, the flowers so high, they could hide from each other. But Ardil had stopped coming with him once he moved to the khan's friend's house. Now Razaq understood why. He felt the regret of not being a better friend to Ardil, but how could he have known?

He had another thought. If he hadn't left the mountains, he wouldn't have seen Tahira. Was it worth it all to have met her? He mentally shook his head, but at least she was a light in a dark place. She was the only thing that had stopped him from shutting off every part of his mind for good. His father would have said she brightened his eyes.

He picked up Mrs. Mumtaz's order from the bakery and was on his way back when he heard someone call his name. Was it Bilal? He hadn't done anything wrong that he could think of, unless Neelma was up to her tricks. He glanced behind him and saw a boy with a jaunty cap on the back of his head. "Zakim?"

Zakim reached him and grinned. "Knew I'd find you one day, Chandi."

"How did you?" Shame that he hadn't returned for Zakim welled up, and he made to turn away.

"You're in my beat, Chandi. This is not far from Moti Bazaar."

Razaq nodded tiredly. "I can't stop," he said. "I have to take these pastries back."

Zakim narrowed his eyes at him. "What's happened to you?"

Razaq shrugged.

"So you are on the streets now? You should come back. You didn't get beaten when you were with me."

Razaq didn't know what to say. If he was gone too long, Mrs. Mumtaz would question him or send Bilal to find him.

"Someone's skewered you, haven't they?"

Razaq's nod was involuntary.

"That happened to me, too. Twice, by men I didn't know."

Razaq wondered what just twice would feel like—he couldn't remember. He frowned. "You smile about it?"

"What else is there to do? Where are you living?"

"I can't say."

"Chandi —"

Razaq turned on him. "I am a slave—don't you understand? I can't even piss in the latrine when I feel like it. They only let me go to the bakery because they know I won't run."

Zakim frowned. "I find that hard to believe. You fought a bear and won, remember."

An image of Tahira rose before Razaq's eyes. She was his Moti.

"There is nothing that can be done now except work to pay them off," he said.

"Chandi? Is this you? Something always can be done."

Razaq walked away. "Not this time."

"Wait. There is a man—he's been asking for months for a green-eyed mountain boy in Moti Bazaar. Chandi, look at me."

Razaq turned.

"I saw your uncle. He came to the scrap yard."

The hollowness in Razaq's heart should have frightened him, but it didn't. He had heard about uncle-seeing before, and he wouldn't fall for that story again.

"It is too late," he said. Let Zakim decide what he meant.

166

When he glanced behind him, Zakim was standing where he had left him, watching the way he went.

❉

The next morning, Razaq woke to the sound of wailing in the house. Then came a quiet knock at his door. It was Tahira. She stood there with tears running down her face; she didn't even bother to wipe them away.

"What is the matter?" he asked. "Why is everyone upset?"

"It is Ismat," she said. "She died."

"How?"

Horrible possibilities flooded his mind. If Bilal hadn't come when that man was beating him, he would have died, too.

"She had a shaving knife."

Razaq frowned. "How did she get that?" None of them were allowed knives. Bilal even had permission to personally search the girls for forbidden objects if he felt it was needed.

"A customer gave it to her. She told him she wanted to shave for him."

Tahira looked embarrassed, perhaps at what Razaq would think, but nothing could embarrass him anymore. He didn't ask how the man had smuggled the knife into the house. Hadn't a customer got a baton into his room without difficulty?

He sighed. "Afsos, I am sorry to hear that."

Tahira nodded. "She was nice to me, but she had lost all hope." She burst into sobbing, and Razaq drew her into his room. After a while, she looked up and touched his face. "Look at you. I heard you had been beaten, and still you have scars. I was sorry I couldn't come. If I didn't have you as

167

my friend, I would be as lost as Ismat. She had no one." Her eyes filled again but she kept talking. "We are disappearing. Every time I dance, it is eating a little more of me away. Soon there will be nothing left. Yesterday Neelma called me a gashtee, a whore, and it is true."

The force of feeling in Razaq's chest jolted him. It was the way he had felt when the boar charged Seema. That day he had a gun, but he had nothing to help Tahira.

"You are not a whore. Inside your heart you are pure." He said it as if he could defy the jinns.

"But they are changing who we are. One day, I will wake up and find that is all I am—a prostitute. Ismat knew this and she couldn't take it any more."

Razaq tried something else. "You have your holy words."

Perhaps he looked worried for she said, "I couldn't do as Ismat has, but I feel so dirty now. Can God forgive this when I can't stop doing it? In the Injil there is a prostitute who Yesu Masih forgives, but she leaves her way of life and becomes his devotee. I can't leave this way of life. I am happy now that my parents are dead—if they knew what I do here they would be heartbroken."

Never had she sounded so bitter.

"Surely God will forgive," Razaq said, but he wondered if he was saying the words as he would to one of his sisters if she broke a glass bangle. Could God truly forgive him for what he willingly did to keep Tahira and himself safe? Or should he be taking more of a risk to escape?

There had to be something they could hang onto. He wanted to say they should fight, but he had lost his fighting spirit, like Ardil had. There was one thing he could say, though he wondered if he could believe it himself.

"We must not let them take our minds as well. Remember who you were. You are still that person."

She shook her head. "It hurts too much. What I was then and what I am now is too different."

She sounded so desolate that Razaq did something he hadn't before. He drew her close and held her against him. It hurt his ribs to stretch his arms around her. He tried to feel brotherly, but that didn't work: hugging his sisters had never felt like this. He knew that if he could hold her all day, he would have the strength to draw back his spirit that was disappearing.

"I don't care whether you are a gashtee or a princess, you are still Tahira."

She stood back a step but he left his hands on her arms.

"Thank you," she said simply. There were still tears in her eyes but her expression had changed; her eyes were shining. "My mother said that all we have to do is believe in Yesu and we will go to heaven, our sin all gone. But we have to say sorry." Her eyes clouded again.

Razaq saw what he could say. "Then ask for forgiveness every day."

Her eyes brightened a little, and he smiled. He wished he could believe something so simple and sure, but he knew he had only the mercy of God to rely on. Maybe he would go to Paradise, maybe not—no one could presume on God's good will. But if he could help Tahira feel better, it was all he wanted.

It was then he looked up and saw Neelma watching him as she walked past his open doorway. Had she seen him hold Tahira?

"You should go," he whispered. "Neelma walked past."

Tahira nodded and adjusted her shawl. She backed out of his room and hurried into the courtyard and to her own room. Razaq watched her go, hoping Neelma hadn't seen him touch her. He could argue he was just being brotherly, but Neelma was unpredictable like her aunt: if something upset her, he never knew which way she would react.

❄

He didn't have long to wait. That afternoon there was a bang on his door, and Mrs. Mumtaz burst into his room.

"Neelma tells me you kissed her. On the mouth." She narrowed her gaze at him. "Where did you learn that disgusting American habit? Films? Or did a customer show you?"

Razaq shook his head. He stood to face her and saw Neelma behind her. What was Neelma's strategy? Had she mentioned Tahira? It didn't seem like it. Was kissing Neelma worse than touching Tahira in Mrs. Mumtaz's eyes, or did Neelma also want to have a hold over him? Do what I say or I will tell about Tahira also? Razaq shuddered. He doubted Mrs. Mumtaz would believe him if he denied it.

"You think you're a mountain stud ram, is that it?" Mrs. Mumtaz sneered at him.

Razaq found it hard to hold his tongue, but he managed it. He could feel the anger rise.

"A beating will do you no good, it seems. Besides, I need you to start work tomorrow. So, no more dancing with the girls in the evenings."

Razaq tried not to look relieved.

"And," Mrs. Mumtaz stared at him so intently her eyes bulged, "no going on the roof or where you can run into the girls, and no more jaunts to the bakery. I've been too easy on you." She stared at him with her face tilted to the side.

Razaq felt the blood rush from his head. How would he cope again stuck in this room all day every day? Not being able to feel the breeze on the roof, or even to go to the latrine; having to do his business before the jamadarni came to empty his bucket? He could feel the walls closing in on him at the thought of it.

He ventured a question. "For how long?" His voice cracked and Mrs. Mumtaz frowned at him.

Then she smirked. "I'll decide what to do with you and how long it will be. For now it is indefinitely."

Razaq glanced at Neelma. Her face had fallen, so he guessed her plan had backfired. What had she expected her aunt to do? Turn him over to her? If Neelma came to his room now, surely Mrs. Mumtaz would know it was Neelma's fault and not his.

But Razaq didn't feel pleased for long that Neelma had been thwarted, not when he heard the bolt on his door slam across. He lay gingerly on his bed. All he felt like doing was weeping. His anger had faded again.

He wondered what Mrs. Mumtaz would decide to do. Maybe she would think he was too much trouble and cut him like Bilal. How long would he be cooped up like a chicken in a butcher's cage waiting for the axe?

Chapter 25

Javaid let himself into work early and sat at the desk. He took out his notebook and booted up the computer. This was now his daily ritual: to contact those organizations that helped rescue and rehabilitate enslaved children. He sent his usual group e-mail to a collection of government agencies asking if a boy called Abdur-Razaq Khan had arrived in their programs. The answers were always the same: "We are sorry, janab, your nephew has not been found." Yet still Javaid persisted.

This morning when he called a nongovernment agency, a man told him they could do nothing without knowledge of Razaq's whereabouts. "If we have some indication of where he is, janab, we can send personnel."

Javaid ended the call and sat staring at the computer screen. What did the man think he had been doing all these months? He had searched so long for Razaq, but it was an impossible task.

His only hope had come from that boy at the scrap yard. He had looked the streetwise sort of boy who could do anything, but Javaid was a fool for trusting him. It had been weeks since he'd seen him at the yard. Maybe the boy had known nothing after all. That policeman had been right: it was up to Javaid to find Razaq. He couldn't give up, even if it took ten calls every day. Surely one day a person would have seen his nephew.

He turned a page in the notebook and rang another number. There was just enough time before Waqar came to work. Javaid was waiting on the line when he heard Zaid arguing with someone outside the shop. It was his duty to keep the young salesmen in line when Waqar wasn't in. He canceled the call, pocketed his notebook and cell phone, and walked to the door.

"What is the matter?" he asked Zaid, barely keeping the annoyance out of his tone.

"It is just another beggar. He says his name is Zakim, and he knows you." Zaid frowned at Javaid. "I am just getting rid of him, but he is most insistent."

Zaid moved and Javaid could see who the beggar was. It was the boy from the scrap yard.

"I'll handle this," he said to Zaid. "You look after the shop."

Zaid brushed past him, grumbling about beggars, and left them alone.

At first, Javaid didn't speak. Zakim was staring at him, the outrage at being called a beggar evident in his stance and raised chin.

"Have you found Razaq?" Javaid finally said. He held his breath, not daring to hope.

Zakim inclined his head and Javaid let his breath out with a whoosh.

"Where?"

The boy looked troubled. "Qasai Gali."

"But that is near here," Javaid said, feeling a rush of excitement. Then he frowned. "Wasn't that once a street of brothels?"

"Ji, janab, and Razaq is in a very difficult situation. It is too dangerous to free him."

Chapter 26

Razaq's afternoons and evenings were soon busy again. He was inundated; it seemed his customers had missed him. It still hurt to bend over the bed during a massage, or to work hard on a man's back, but his ribs were gradually healing. Bilal had been given the job of cutting his stitches and pulling them out. Razaq wondered if Bilal spoke to the customers before they came in because for weeks no one asked for "whatever." It gave Razaq more time to heal.

One customer said how sorry he was to hear an evil man had beaten him. "You shouldn't be working here," he said. "You should work on your own, and you can decide which customers you want. If you do this, let me know, and I will come to you there."

Razaq said nothing. It was a good idea, but he realized the man didn't know his circumstances. How many of his customers didn't understand he was a slave? Did they think he chose to live this way?

If Mrs. Mumtaz had wanted to wound him even more than a beating, she had succeeded. Razaq hated being a prisoner in his room. If he woke too early, he paced the small area beside his bed. Then he stood at the window and stared out between the bars. At least he had that, even if he couldn't see the sun rise or set. He watched the food wallahs pushing their carts filled with vegetables, saw Bilal head off toward the bazaar. Once Bilal glanced back and lifted an arm. Could he see Razaq there?

Razaq searched the gali for Zakim, but there was no sign of him. He thought about what Zakim had said about a man asking for him. Would Zakim make up such a thing? Why should he? He didn't answer to anyone like Aslam did. But what could be done?

Razaq picked his pakol off the hook on the wall and turned it in circles in his hands as he thought. This hat showed who he was and where he came from—a mountain boy, free and strong. He closed his eyes. He was neither of those things any more. He was the shadow a wounded wolf made as it slunk through the jungle, an ill-treated dog with no spirit even to wag its tail as it sat sad eyed with its nose on its paws. Razaq groaned and threw the hat in the corner. It just missed the latrine bucket.

He sat on the bed, stood again. He had to keep off the bed. If he lay down, he would curl up and sleep like a baby until his first customer came. He had to make himself think. He thought of his father and the day he had taken him to a forest up the mountain. It took half the day to trek there. It was cool; Razaq had a shawl wrapped around him, and he carried his gun over his shoulder like his father did. They were tracking game when Razaq saw two men in the distance. He heard a shot, but when he and his father reached the place, there was a dead bear left on the ground.

"Why did they kill her and not take the carcass?" Razaq asked.

His father told him men killed mother bears to capture the cubs.

A year later, a man had brought a young bear into the village. It had a rope through its nose. It danced during the day, but after dancing it had to face two ferocious dogs. Razaq's father forbade him to watch. Uncle Javaid said bear baiting was wrong. So did his father.

"I may be uneducated, unlike your uncle, but I am not ignorant," he said to Razaq.

Razaq remembered the bloody nose of the bear. He had seen the cage that the bear had to sleep in. To a bear it would have seemed as small as this room did to him.

Razaq heard the bolt drawn back. His door opened and Bilal stood there, a grin on his face. "I've brought someone to meet you." He pushed a boy into the room.

Razaq started in surprise. "Danyal?"

The boy didn't smile.

"Is it you?" Razaq took a step closer and the boy flinched. Razaq stopped. Where was the cheeky boy full of Punjabi jokes from Mr. Malik's house? He glanced up at Bilal.

"He has been trained as a malishia, like you," Bilal said. "Mrs. M has found malish is good for business."

Razaq tried not to stare at Danyal. What had happened to him? Had he himself also changed that much? Then a thought struck Razaq. Now Ismat was gone, a room was spare. Was Danyal his replacement should he cause Mrs. Mumtaz any further trouble?

As if Bilal could read his thoughts, he said, "Mrs. M told me to bring him so you know he is here. Maybe you have some malish tips for him?"

Razaq blew out a breath. What hadn't he known at first? "Whatever," but by the look of Danyal, he had been taught that lesson already. What would he have liked someone to tell him? He knew Mrs. Mumtaz would want him to explain the rules: to not cause trouble, do "whatever," don't touch the girls or you get locked up.

Instead, he said, "Do not let them take your whole self, Danyal—remember your jokes in your mind."

Danyal spoke then. "What good will that do? Will it help me escape?"

Razaq thought about that. "No, it won't change what happens to you, but it could make you think differently about how you feel. They are the ones who have given us these feelings of dirt and shame. We have mushkil, difficult feelings, now, but we are the same inside." He thought of Zakim saying he answered to no man and laid a hand over his chest. "Don't let them break you in here."

Danyal stared at him as if he were crazy.

Razaq suddenly grinned. Perhaps he was. Would he have been able to say that if he didn't have Tahira to think about? But he knew he was truly telling himself these things. Certainly, he was locked in a room, but he wasn't dead yet. He may still think of something.

❋

Late one afternoon, a strange man came for a massage. Razaq stared at the man's dark trousers and white shirt. He rarely had customers who wore Angrezi clothes.

"My name is Majeed," the man said. "You do massages?"

Customers rarely gave their name either. Razaq tipped his head to the side.

The man was checking out his room. "What else do you do here?"

Razaq's legs sagged, but he said with the emotion of a stone, "Whatever you want."

Majeed said, "Look at me. Razaq, is it not? I have heard of you."

A hot feeling grew up Razaq's back. What did he mean?

The man was watching him intently. "I do not want anything from you."

Razaq didn't know whether to believe him or not; every muscle in his body was tensed. What if the man attacked him like the last crazy man? He would be ready this time.

"Malishias don't usually work in chaklas. Are you working here of your own free will? Or are you working off a debt?" When Razaq didn't respond, he said, "Would you not rather work as a malishia on your own?"

Was it some trick of Mrs. Mumtaz's to check his loyalty? Razaq chewed the inside of his cheek. If he said "yes," Majeed might complain. Then Mrs. Mumtaz would have a reason to cut him. She wanted to, he could tell. Even his voice was betraying him lately: squeaky one minute, cracking like a man's the next. If she cut him, he wouldn't grow a beard; he would have a voice like Bilal's and always be a boy for her customers. He would never marry Tahira.

The man took a card from his pocket. "Here, keep this. Call me and I will bring help if you want me to."

If it wasn't so frightening it would be funny. Razaq closed his eyes. Next thing Majeed would be saying he had seen Zakim or someone he knew. He stood straighter, put the card on the bed; he had to stay strong.

"By the way," the man said, "do you have a relative called Javaid Khan?"

If Razaq had been holding the card, he would have dropped it. His breath came faster. Majeed was clever like a fox and Razaq didn't dare open his mouth in case he was tricked into saying something he shouldn't.

"Call me." Majeed held his thumb and little finger to his ear to look like a phone as he went out of the door.

Razaq slumped onto the bed. He couldn't trust the man, he couldn't. Then a voice inside his head said, *Who knows you have an uncle?*

Mrs. Mumtaz didn't know he had an uncle, did she? Who had he told? Aslam, Zakim, Tahira. Had he told Bilal? He couldn't remember. Would Bilal betray him? Bilal worked for Mrs. Mumtaz and his first loyalty was to her. Suddenly, he stood up. Had Mrs. Mumtaz hurt Tahira to make her tell? He made himself calm down. It didn't make sense for anyone to want to find that out.

He turned the card over in his hand. He had seen cards like this: businessmen gave them to each other. There was an orange splash of color on the card, a star. It was so long since he had seen a book or a picture. Razaq sighed. That simple star, it was a light. His Uncle Javaid had told him once that people were like colored windows: when the sun was out, they shone easily; but when the darkness set in, their true beauty was only revealed if there was light from within. Zakim had said Razaq had a light within. Did he still have that?

He looked at the card again. He couldn't read it all; the letters were strange. He sounded out Majeed's name, and there were numbers—his phone number obviously. Razaq grunted. Majeed didn't know much. Where would he get a phone? Majeed didn't even know he was locked in this room.

When Bilal brought Razaq's curry and bread, Razaq shoved the card in his shalwar pocket.

Bilal had two white cords stuck in his ears. When he saw Razaq staring, he pulled them out. "It's an iPod. I can listen anytime even when I go to the bazaar."

"A what?"

Bilal showed Razaq the white plastic box smaller than a cell phone. "Here, you try." He shoved the white buds into Razaq's ears. It made him grin. Bilal pulled a bud out. "It is Bollywood music. Amir Khan."

"I like his acting," Razaq said. "He always wins his fights."

"The hero always wins—that's Bollywood." Bilal laughed but Razaq could hear the yearning underneath. He sighed.

It was a good feeling having music fill his head; there was little room left for any thoughts of his own. No wonder Bilal wore it all day.

Razaq took out the cords and handed them back. "Shukriya."

Bilal was putting the iPod back in his pocket when Razaq asked his question. "Did you tell Mrs. Mumtaz I have an uncle?"

Bilal looked up with such surprise that Razaq knew what he said would be true. "No, why give her bullets to fire?" Then he said with a frown, "Do you have an uncle?"

Razaq regarded Bilal. Should he tell him about Majeed and laugh with him about what a crazy man he was? But he decided against it. If Majeed was telling the truth, the less Bilal knew the better.

Chapter 27

Razaq stood at the bottom of the mountain. It was made of black rock and stretched to the heavens. His mother put a wolf-skin vest on him and strapped sheepskins to his legs and feet. She put his pakol on his head and wrapped a goat's-hair shawl around his neck and shoulders. "Make me proud to be the mother of Abdur-Razaq Nadeem Khan," she whispered. "You are the only one who can fight the jinn and save the mountain. Climb to the top and the curse will be broken."

He jumped up to the first foothold and hauled himself higher like the Angrez mountain climbers did, except he had no ropes. Whenever he wavered, his mother's voice was in his head. "Fight, Razaq, fight the tiredness. There is no mountain you cannot climb."

His hands were like claws finding rocks to hold onto. His feet followed his hands. He squinted up at the top. It never seemed to get any closer, but he knew he had to keep going. His father always said that mountain men were like the mountains themselves—they never gave up, never let anything conquer them, whether it be the government or militants or harsh living conditions.

When he managed to reach the top, the wind knocked him backward, but he stood his ground and saw in front of him not the other side of the black rock mountain but green land sloping down to the valley and river below. When he looked behind him, the black rock dissolved before his eyes and became the forest he knew.

Razaq's eyes flew open. He had been dreaming, but he didn't mind. Some days it was as if he truly was in the mountains: he could see his mother's eyes telling him he was special, her only son, the one who would carry on his father's name. He would have looked after his parents in their old age, his sisters too if they were widowed; grown apricot trees on the slopes. Razaq sighed. That was before the earthquake.

Why hadn't he resisted Ikram? Why hadn't he realized he was an evil man? It had all happened so fast. If he had been able to say good-bye to Hussain and Abdul, they would have known—they were older, had seen more of life. But Ikram wouldn't let him. Wasn't that when he should have realized?

Razaq held his head in his hands and groaned. He couldn't live like this forever. He just couldn't. He was just like Ardil. No one would give his daughter in marriage to a boy who had been involved in bachabazi like Ardil or prostitution as Razaq was. He knew a man keeping a boy like Ardil in his home was haram, and yet other men must have known it was going on. How was it that a man could be whipped for committing adultery, a woman stoned even, but a rich, important man could ruin a boy's life and still walk free? Like Mr. Malik.

Razaq clenched his fingers. What had he to look forward to here? Nothing. He couldn't even see Tahira. Bilal and his iPod was the only good part of his day, but he knew he couldn't fully trust Bilal, just as he hadn't been able to trust Aslam.

He closed his eyes, trying to picture his mother again in his mind. If he could only keep her with him maybe he could endure. But she faded as she always did. His mother had told him to take notice of dreams, for it was the way God spoke. Razaq sat up, his eyes wide open. He sat still on the edge of the bed for a long time, and then he knew what he had to do.

The first customer that day was one of his regulars who needed a back massage. He was a bank teller, one of the few customers who wore Angrezi clothes. After the session was finished and the man was buttoning up his shirt, Razaq took a risk. He chewed the inside of his cheek and then blurted out, "Do you have a cell phone?"

He knew the man did; everyone owned one, it seemed, except him. Even Bilal had one so Mrs. Mumtaz could contact him.

"Certainly," the man said. "You need to make a call?"

Razaq gave the ghost of a smile and nodded. The man showed the same hospitality his parents had instilled in him: if someone asks for help, you give it. He watched as the man reached into his pocket. He had to be careful. What if he had misjudged the man, and he told Mrs. Mumtaz that Razaq had used his phone? It would probably be an offense worthy of being cut.

The man handed Razaq the phone. Razaq had memorized the number; he didn't want anyone seeing that card. He tried to look businesslike, but he had no idea how to use the phone.

The man smiled. "This way," he said and turned the phone around. "Touch the keypad here and speak in there." He pointed so Razaq could see.

Razaq pressed the numbers and was surprised by the keypad tones, then he put the phone to his ear as the man indicated. When Majeed answered, Razaq said, "Janab, I can fit you in today if you wish. It is Razaq." He didn't wait for Majeed to say anything and handed the phone back.

The man pressed a key on the phone and smiled at Razaq as he put it in his pocket. Razaq wasn't sure what the smile meant. Did the man think he had a special relationship? More importantly, did the man know that only Mrs. Mumtaz made bookings and would he tell? Razaq tried to appear calm. Never show a dangerous animal you have fear—look uninterested.

"Khuda hafiz, good-bye," he said to the customer at the door, then he sank onto the bed. Mrs. Mumtaz was always swift to act. If the man saw her and mentioned the incident, Razaq wouldn't have long to wait. If the man told Bilal, who normally showed customers out and locked Razaq's door again, would he tell Mrs. Mumtaz? Razaq sat holding his knees, rocking with his thoughts.

There was a bang on the door. Razaq jumped off the bed and stood by the window. The door opened and Bilal ushered in a customer, another of Razaq's regulars. Bilal gave him a strange look, and Razaq hoped it was only because he was standing by the window like a frightened lamb.

It was difficult to concentrate on the man's massage. Razaq's mind wobbled all over the place. He had done such a dangerous thing: raced downwind into the path of a she-bear. Would she notice?

Majeed didn't come that day, nor the next. Maybe the phone didn't work. Maybe that was why the customer had smiled: he had tricked Razaq. Or maybe Majeed was too busy for him. He was a fool to think anyone might care about children locked in a brothel.

It was Bilal who put an end to his torment. "I have something for you," he said with a grin. It was a folded piece of paper.

Razaq couldn't think. Surely Majeed hadn't contacted Bilal? Had he been caught out? But if so, why was Bilal looking so smug?

"It is from a girl," Bilal teased.

This did nothing to reassure Razaq. Neelma would be just the sort of girl to write a note to a boy, and he didn't need trouble from her right now.

"You look like a wild animal is chasing you," Bilal said. "Here." He handed it over.

Razaq hesitated before unfolding the page. What he saw was a picture of a mountain, a sun, and goats climbing on rocks. It was a child's picture. He raised his eyebrows at Bilal.

"It's from Tahira. To cheer you up."

Razaq looked more closely. The thicker lines were made of what appeared to be little squiggles, but he could tell they were letters. He grinned at Bilal.

"Just a bit of scribble, but she said it would brighten your eyes." A knowing look came over Bilal's face. "I can see it worked. You like her, don't you?"

Razaq gave the stock answer to such a question: "She is like a sister." He shrugged, hoping Bilal would let it drop.

"Don't let Mrs. M know," Bilal said, as he left.

It is too late for that, Razaq thought. Mrs. Mumtaz knew from the beginning. How else could she keep such a hold over him?

Razaq fingered the picture made up of Urdu squiggles. How clever Tahira had been. No one would know that she could write or he could read. It took him a while, but he worked it out. *Tu kia hai,* she had written, *how are you? Kash ke hum millen, I wish we could meet.* The note did as much for Razaq as the dream had.

Was it just a dream to think he and Tahira could marry? Could they even have a normal relationship? He thought of his parents. He was old enough to realize his father had shared his mother's bed sometimes; had heard their low whispers when they thought he was asleep, his father's chuckle, their embracing. That was what he wanted with Tahira, but would everything that had happened to them flood their minds every time they tried to dance?

He groaned—he had to think of a different word. Love. Could love cover the dirt and shame he carried daily in his mind and body?

Chapter 28

When Majeed did visit, Razaq wasn't even expecting it. He had to think quickly for a few seconds who the man standing in front of him was.

"Razaq? Are you okay?"

"I didn't think you would come."

Majeed stepped further into the room. He stood so close to him, Razaq had to steel himself not to step backward. He had decided to trust this man if he returned.

Majeed's smile was sad and he spoke softly. "I am truly sorry. There is always much to do. So many children . . ." He stopped and glanced back at the door. "I can bring some good men from the Protection Center—supporters who work against the trafficking of children—and a good policeman to take you to a safe place."

Razaq cut in: "There is someone else here."

"It works best if we only have one of you to worry about at a time."

"Then I want you to take a girl. She is only twelve—" Razaq checked himself, "Maybe thirteen now, but she is the youngest here." He thought of Danyal, but shut his mouth. It would be good to get everyone out, but Majeed sounded busy. "Can you see her?"

He paused. Would Majeed want to dance with Tahira once he saw her? She was very pretty. No, Majeed wore a different expression on his face than most of the men who came to the chakla. "Her name is Tahira."

"What about you?" Majeed said. "We could take you and come back for her. Someone wants to see you."

Majeed must mean his uncle, but Razaq clamped his heart shut. "I could not go and leave her here," he said simply.

"Then we will try to get you both out. She is not your sister?"

Razaq shook his head. He knew it was possible Majeed wouldn't bother with Tahira if he said she wasn't, but he stood his ground. "I love her as much as a sister. We were in another house together."

Majeed's eyes widened. "A training house?"

Razaq nodded.

"You can tell me where this house is?"

Razaq hesitated. "Inshallah, after we are away from here."

Majeed smiled then. "Accha, I see you haven't lost your spirit."

Razaq thought about that. Before the dream of climbing the mountain, he had felt like a captive wolf, frustrated and hopeless. Maybe a little of his spirit had returned after all.

"You will know when we come," Majeed said. "Just be ready." He turned to face Razaq again before he opened the door. "It may take some time, so do not lose hope." Then he whispered Tahira's name.

Razaq inclined his head to show he had said it correctly.

When the door closed, Razaq didn't know whether he had been clever or a fool. What if he had put Tahira into more danger? He pulled out the picture she had drawn. There was a space at the bottom. He folded the paper and carefully ripped that piece off. He should have asked Majeed for a pencil. Would Bilal bring him one? He thought about what he would write. He would have to do it as a picture, too. He would draw the mountains with his letters rising to the top, ready to soar off the paper. He would tell her Majeed was coming; to go with him.

❄

When Bilal brought dinner, Razaq asked him for a pencil.

"Where would I get a pencil?" Bilal said.

"One of the girls?" Razaq knew Tahira must have one but didn't want to remind Bilal about Tahira. He changed the subject. "Where is Danyal's room?"

Bilal glanced at him. "Ismat's old room, near Tahira's. Why? You thinking of breaking out of here and visiting him?"

Razaq tried to grin at the joke, but felt as if he had been shot like a wild goat eating his father's crop.

Bilal sat on the bed and pulled out his pouch of cigarette papers. He had an assortment of tobacco, paan, and other things Razaq wasn't sure of. "Here, share this with me. It will get you through the evening. You won't feel a thing."

"I won't massage so well either," Razaq said.

Bilal blew smoke in the air and a sickly smell hung around Razaq's head. Razaq had smelled that before in the mountains, when he had passed men sitting together over a hookah.

"How will I get rid of the stink?" he said.

"Mrs. M won't mind. How do you think she gets the new girls to lie still for the customers?"

Razaq thought back to the few times he had seen Tahira. Her eyes had seemed unfocused at times. He hoped Majeed

189

came soon. The men he had known who smoked hashish or opium in the mountains were very soon controlled by it. His father used to say men like that couldn't make a decision unless they consulted the hookah pipe first.

"Razaq?" Bilal shoved him playfully. "You're far away today."

Razaq held his head in his hands. "I am sick of being locked up. I wish the police would come and close the chakla."

"Ha. The police are some of Mrs. M's best customers, except they don't pay—she pays them when they visit." Bilal tipped his head and grimaced as Razaq looked at him. "I feel bad for you. It is not good for anyone to be locked up, but kissing Neelma?" He made a stupid face.

"You believe that?"

Bilal stared at him, his lips pursed. "So it is like that, is it?"

"It is best not to say anything," Razaq said quickly. "Neelma will just think of something worse."

He thought of the hug he had given Tahira. It was a dangerous thing to have done.

Bilal nodded. "I don't think Mrs. M is fooled by Neelma, otherwise she would have—" He made a chopping motion with his hand.

"Then why lock me up?"

Bilal searched his face, then blew smoke in it. "Maybe she thinks bushes don't shake without wind."

Razaq felt a cold shiver come over him. What did Bilal know?

Then Bilal laughed. "What could you get up to locked in a room?" He handed over the iPod. "Here, have a turn while I am here."

It took Bilal a day to find a pencil. He also brought another note from Tahira. He dropped onto the bed and and rested his back against the wall. "If I thought you two could truly write, I would have to report it to Mrs. M."

Razaq stared Bilal steadily in the face. "It is just scribbling and a picture, as you can see. She doesn't have much to keep her happy. I thought I would do one back. Would you not do the same for your sister?"

Bilal didn't speak for a moment, then he inclined his head. "I had a sister. I hope she is happy." Then he added quietly, "I hope she thinks I am dead."

Razaq sighed. He knew what Bilal meant. "I am sorry. All of mine died in the earthquake."

Bilal glanced at him. "So that's why you like Tahira."

Razaq lifted his chin. Let Bilal think that, although he knew there was more to it. When he had hugged his sisters goodnight, it had never felt like holding Tahira did. He drew his mountains for Tahira.

"Accha, nice picture," Bilal said, watching over his shoulder. "You must miss those mountains. I would have liked to see them."

Razaq heard the wistfulness in Bilal's tone. He understood that note of finality, too, as if Bilal had come to the end of his life. It was how he had felt a few days ago. He kept quiet; empty words like "Inshallah, one day you will" would have been insensitive.

"Was there snow?" Bilal had another cigarette rolling in his fingers.

Razaq smiled. "Much snow in the winter; now it would be melting in the lower areas."

"How did you keep warm in your house?"

"I made a fire in a hollow in the dried mud floor. My mother cooked over it and this warmed the whole room. We had no windows—that helped to keep the cold out. We did everything in that room—ate, slept, told stories at night. If men came to visit Abu, they sat outside with a fire."

"Lakes? Rivers?"

"Zarur, certainly. It took many hours to climb down to the village above the Indus. But there was a quicker way. To cross the mountain stream."

"A bridge?"

Razaq shook his head. "There are no bridges in Kala Dhaka. A basket with a rope. You pull yourself across."

"That sounds dangerous." Bilal finished his cigarette and threw the stub in Razaq's bucket.

"Ji. Lots of things are dangerous in the mountains. Guns, wild dogs, bears, the Indus if you fall in." Razaq's voice grew quiet as he added, "And earthquakes."

Maybe it was the talk of what they had lost that made Bilal say no more about pictures and scribbles; he just took Razaq's piece of paper. "I will give this to your little sister, bhai." It was the first time Bilal had called him "brother."

"Shukriya," Razaq murmured with his right hand over his heart.

Chapter 29

Weeks went by and Razaq went through the motions of his life, thinking about the stupid thing he had done. Every time his door banged open, he jumped, only to find it was Bilal with dinner or the shaver. He thought about the fear that had him in its jaws. It was true that terrible things happened, but if he could only change his thoughts, the fear would have less hold over him. It was the same idea that he had tried to explain to Danyal. It was like tracking a wolf: he couldn't show fear or the wolf would sense it, but it didn't mean he wasn't afraid. His father had told him that was what courage truly was. "Which man does not feel fear?" he had said once. "But the courageous man is not bound by it. He does what he has to regardless."

Razaq didn't dare think of his uncle and how he wouldn't want him when he knew all about him. Majeed had promised him a safe place, and it was that safety he wanted for Tahira. Maybe with Tahira gone, he could escape by himself, join Zakim. Though who knew how Mrs. Mumtaz's rage would manifest. It would be like a bomb exploding. Surely she would realize he was behind the raid when it happened. If it ever happened. Razaq sighed.

He was between customers and it was getting late when he heard a commotion in the dancing room. "Razaq!" It was Tahira.

He slammed up against his door. It shook, but didn't give: it was still bolted on the outside. What was happening to her?

Then he heard a man's voice. "Razaq!" *Majeed.* He still didn't know Razaq was locked in.

Razaq rested his head against the door. At least Tahira would leave. It was a pity Majeed had called his name for now Mrs. Mumtaz would know for sure the part he had played.

Then he heard a slight noise above the raised voices heading outside. A scratch on his door, the sound of a bolt being slowly and carefully drawn. Razaq pulled open the door. Danyal stood there, a grin on his face that made him look like his old cocky self.

"What have you done?" Razaq whispered.

"No one will know it was me. Look."

They both stared out the front door. Majeed had Tahira by the hand. There were three policemen and two other official-looking men with him. Mrs. Mumtaz was trying to shove money in their faces.

"Come with me," Razaq said.

Danyal shook his head. "I wouldn't be fast enough. Someone has tipped off Mr. Malik; Murad is here. He has a pistol."

Razaq quickly checked the group outside.

"Tahira is safe," Danyal added. "Murad keeps away from policemen who won't take bribes."

Mrs. Mumtaz was walking up the steps, cursing. Razaq had left it too late. He dashed toward the courtyard, while

Danyal bolted his door. Razaq took the steps to the roof three at a time. He ached from not exercising, but he would have to be a mountain goat this night. He checked behind him, but Danyal wasn't there. He reached the roof and ran along it to jump across a narrow gali to the next roof. Sooner or later the buildings would surely change to single story and he could slide to the ground.

"Stop!" It was Bilal. He was right behind him—how did he get there so quickly?

Razaq could hear Mrs. Mumtaz's screams of rage in the courtyard. There were other footsteps too. Then a shot. He heard the zing. *Murad.*

Razaq kept running along the roofs, weaving in case Murad shot at him again. He couldn't stop. If Bilal caught him, he would have to hand him over to Mrs. Mumtaz. The streetlights made him an easy target for Murad. There was nothing for it: he would have to go over the edge. How much different from slithering down a steep mountain slope could it be?

He looked down to the gali below, glanced back at Bilal. He was too close. Razaq crouched to his hands and knees and slipped over the side. He checked for a foothold between the cement bricks and found one. He was just about to move his hands down when his right hand was grabbed.

"I've got him!" Bilal yelled.

Razaq could feel the thumping of Murad's approaching footsteps through the cement.

"Let me go, bhai," he whispered. "Let me fall."

How far would Bilal's loyalty to Mrs. Mumtaz go? Maybe he would be punished too if Razaq got away.

"He's slipping!" Bilal shouted. "Quickly. I can't hold him."

It wasn't true. Bilal was much stronger than Razaq and could have pulled him up to the roof again.

"Allah go with you," Bilal whispered. Then he opened his hand.

Razaq's feet slid, scrabbling for a hold they couldn't find, until they landed against a top window ledge. There was a bottom ledge on his window in Mrs. Mumtaz's house; he hoped there was one here, too. He stretched one arm down and grabbed a bar as he slid down. Yes, there was another ledge. He rested his feet on it and looked up. There were two silhouettes against the night sky. Was Murad aiming the gun at him? He couldn't tell.

He let himself slip and hung onto the bottom ledge with his hands a moment. How far from the ground was he? Would he break his legs if he fell? Better than being shot. Just then a bullet skimmed past his head. He heard its squeal and then the thud as it entered the cement farther below.

That decided it. He let go of the ledge and tried to get a grip on the wall, but this time there were no cracks in the cement. His legs and arms flailed as he fell, bumping and scraping against the wall. An awning broke his fall. He bounced off it, crashed to the gali and landed, winded, on his back.

More shots sprayed the ground near him, and he scrambled closer to the building. Nothing felt broken, though his right leg didn't work properly, and he was as sore as if he'd been beaten. His skin burned from all the scrapes. He had been fortunate, but now he needed to reach the bazaar. He crouched and glanced up at the roof. Only one figure stood there now. He guessed Murad would be out in the gali soon to chase him down. It didn't bear imagining what would happen if he was caught.

He forced himself to stand up and half-ran, half-limped down the gali. He stopped a moment to take in a few shuddering breaths. His sides hurt; he felt as if his heart would rip apart.

He heard a shout and urged himself to move again, but a sharp pain shot up his leg. Maybe one of his bones was broken after all. It seemed as if only a minute had passed when he heard another shout. It sounded like his name. There was a scuffle further behind him. Then a shot. He pushed himself on. Maybe Bilal was fighting Murad. If so, Razaq could be of little help; and what if he went back and Bilal was forced to hand him over to Murad? He couldn't waste this opportunity now that Tahira was safe.

Then he paused. Bilal had called him brother, had saved his life, and given him his freedom. He turned and limped back the way he had come. He wasn't sure what he could do, but he had to try.

Two men were fighting in the gali; there was no one else around. Razaq drew closer. It was like watching a wrestling match in the village, except one of these men could die. One man slammed a fist in the other's stomach, and he fell. The man on the ground reached for something; the other man kicked it away. *The gun.* Razaq could see it glinting under the streetlight.

He edged closer and picked it up just as the man on top smashed a fist into the man under him. The grunts of the fight stopped. Razaq still wasn't sure if Murad or Bilal had won. He stood there with the gun in his hand.

The man standing didn't speak. Was it Murad? Razaq tightened his finger on the trigger. Could he shoot a man? His eyes blurred and he wiped them with his left arm.

"Razaq?"

It must be Bilal. He lowered the gun.

"Razaq? It's me."

He shut his eyes. What trick was Bilal trying? The voice sounded familiar: a mountain voice, speaking in Pukhtu. Was he losing his senses?

The voice came closer. "You are safe now."

Warily, he opened his eyes, blinking. For an instant, he thought the man standing before him was his father. But it wasn't. It was Uncle Javaid, with blood running down his face. That wasn't all: his uncle was weeping.

Razaq dropped the gun and fell to the ground to touch his uncle's feet. Javaid lifted him up to face him.

"Razaq, it is you. Thank God, I have found you at last."

Chapter 30

Mrs. Mumtaz burst into the room. In her raised hand was a knife with a long narrow blade. "You will not escape, my mountain wolf. You have ruined my business, but I will keep you a boy forever. You will never escape—you will always work for me."

She turned to the door and pushed a bolt across—it was as loud as a gunshot.

Razaq sat upright, panting. He watched the morning sun peek into his window and remembered where he was. That first night after Majeed and his uncle had brought him to the Protection Center, a woman had showed him to this room.

"It is just to sleep in," the woman said. "You can go outside whenever you like."

How had she known he was afraid of a bolted door?

When Majeed and his uncle had gone, the woman had stayed. There had been a woman at Mr. Malik's house, too, and Razaq didn't relax.

This one smiled kindly. "My name is Parveen. I will not touch you." She said it as if she knew all about him. She looked at his face and the way he limped. "The doctor will come soon."

Razaq stiffened and she added, "You are safe now. This is a good doctor."

Her gaze didn't waver even when Razaq glanced at her sharply. She reminded him of Rebekah, although Rebekah had skin even paler than his and that strange henna-colored hair.

"Is Tahira here?" he asked.

Parveen inclined her head. "You can see her later. The doctor is treating her, and she will need to stay in the surgery for some days."

Razaq couldn't help himself: he felt the heat rise into his face, knew his eyes would look wild like a wolf's. He took a faltering step toward Parveen and his bad leg locked. A pain shot up to his back.

Parveen didn't even flinch; she regarded him steadily. "She is a good doctor."

She?

"It is over, Razaq. You and Tahira are safe."

Parveen was patient as she repeated the word "safe," but Razaq wondered how many times he would need to hear it before he believed. What did safe mean? Were they safe from Mr. Malik and Mrs. Mumtaz? Would he ever be safe from his thoughts?

Then Parveen had said softly, "We will help you with the memories."

Razaq had stared at her, startled.

The doctor had been gentle in setting his ankle. She reminded him of his mother, asking him questions as if she were inquiring about the weather as she put a cast on his leg.

Parveen wrote down Razaq's answers and showed him pictures of houses in Islamabad. Razaq pointed to Mr. Malik's house.

The doctor rested her hand on his cast. "You have been very brave, Razaq."

He knew she wasn't talking of his fractured bone. He wondered if the broken places deep inside him would heal as well as his leg.

After a few days, Parveen took him to a room to eat with other children. There were so many—many more than at Mr. Malik's house. As he entered with his crutch, he stopped, surprised.

"What is it?" Parveen asked.

Razaq indicated a table where younger children were sitting. "I know that girl," he said. It was Moti. Then he saw Raj and Hira.

Moti didn't seem surprised to see him. "Zakim found this safe place for us," she said around a mouthful of egg and paratha.

Razaq grinned. What couldn't Zakim do in Moti's eyes?

"We live here now," Raj said, "and go to school. Zakim visits us."

Razaq could imagine that Zakim would not want to live in an institution.

"That is until someone wants to adopt us," Moti explained.

"Mmm," was all Hira said. She was too busy with her food.

Razaq would have to tell Majeed about Danyal and Aslam. Maybe they could come here, too.

It was a week before Razaq saw Tahira. They sat together at breakfast and hardly said a word. At first, there was nothing to say. It was as if they understood each other's pain more than anyone else in the room could, and it was enough for Razaq to watch her, to know she was safe. The rogue thought snuck into his mind again. Would they ever truly be safe? Would Murad recover and find them, just as Aslam had found him in the scrap yard and Zakim and Majeed had found him in Qasai Gali? He pushed the thought away. He wouldn't let it spoil this day.

"Come outside," he said.

There was a garden and a high wall. Some of the younger children were already there, playing soccer. Sounds of the traffic—rickshaws and cars—floated over from outside but seemed far away.

Tahira was watching him. "Razaq," she said, "thank you."

He felt his face grow hot.

"I am glad you were able to escape, too." She put a finger on his cheek—he knew he had a scab there—and glanced at the cast on his ankle. "I heard you jumped off the roof."

He grinned. "Sort of. All that jumping I did in the mountains chasing goats helped." He didn't say how much form he had lost from being cooped up so long.

"When I feel better, I am going to study at the Christian Girls College in Rawalpindi," Tahira said.

Razaq wondered if they would ever feel better, but he made an effort and said, "I am happy for you." He wished he could touch her. She looked prettier than ever.

"What will you do?" she asked.

Razaq thought of his uncle. They had talked that first night. "I shall live with Uncle Javaid and go to school. Then," he searched her face, "I will return to the mountains, work the land like my father did. Maybe start a different sort of school where girls can learn, like you."

Tahira nodded, and he hoped it would not be difficult to persuade her to join him there. He sighed inwardly; first he needed to tame the dark shadows that lurked in every corner of his mind. Tahira's face clouded as if she were seeing those shadows, too.

"What is the matter?" he asked gently.

"We are getting older. We will not be able to see each other."

Razaq frowned as he thought. "Could we write? Will that be permissable?"

"I hope so. I will live at the school since I have no relatives."

"We know how to send secret messages."

She smiled and her eyes lit her whole face. Razaq caught his breath at the beauty of it. She had never smiled like that before.

"Do not worry about anything," he said. "I am from the mountains, and just as those mountains cannot be moved, I will never forget you." He paused, gazing at her eyes, then quoted a proverb his mother told him. "There is always a way from heart to heart."

Tahira's eyes filled and she put her hand in his. She didn't say a word but the look in her eyes and the warmth of her hand was enough.

❇

Razaq climbed out of bed smiling at the memory of Tahira's eyes promising him all he wanted. Today something else good would happen: Uncle Javaid was coming to take him home. But what if his uncle changed his mind? He'd had a month to decide what a bad idea it would be to bring a boy like Razaq into his house.

When Javaid strode through the door, Razaq almost wept. So many men had come through his door over the last nine months. What he would have given to see his uncle stride into Mr. Malik's house or Mrs. Mumtaz's chakla. A scar on his uncle's face was still red, and there was a crescent on the side of his head where part of his hair had been shaved. Those wounds had been for Razaq.

"I have come to take you home," Javaid said simply.

Razaq stared at him, then voiced his fear. "I thought you wouldn't want me. I am nothing now."

Javaid made a noise with his tongue and Razaq wasn't sure if he was angry with him. Javaid drew closer and laid a hand on Razaq's head in blessing.

"You are Abdur-Razaq Nadeem Khan, my flesh and blood." His voice was strong, just like a mountain man's, even though he had no beard. "And to honor the memory of your father, you will be as my very own son."

Razaq had no words in the face of such love. He gazed at his uncle in disbelief. There were so many things he would never be able to tell him, so many things he'd never forget and wished he could, and yet, looking into his uncle's eyes, it was as if he understood it all.

❋

Nothing had changed with Mrs. Daud. When Javaid brought Razaq to the mud house, she raced toward him and hugged him. "Oh my son, I've been so worried about you." It was as if she knew she had done wrong in letting him go.

"Just call her Auntie-ji," Javaid advised. "Perhaps in time she will become used to being an aunt."

Sakina was the next person Razaq saw. She looked so like Seema that his eyes watered. Now that he was no longer bonded to those evil people, he was thinking more about his family, especially his sisters and his mother who he couldn't save. Tears came more easily now he was safe than they had when he was a slave.

Amina enveloped him in a hug. "You are a gift from God, Razaq. I have always wanted a son," she whispered into his ear. He wept openly for the first time since his release. She would be his mother now. No one could replace his real parents, but he would be a good son to Amina just as his mother had taught him.

Razaq wiped his eyes and let Sakina take his hand. She led him to the courtyard, bent down to a box, and lifted out a chick. She held it out to him. "It is for you." Then she added solemnly, "You are my brother now."

He took the chick and kneeled to hug her. He closed his eyes at the fresh smell of her hair and saw the mountains rising up from the Indus, his mother banging the rug outside, his father cutting grass, his sisters chasing the goats among the wildflowers on the mountain slope.

When he opened his eyes, Sakina was staring at him. She touched the tear rolling down his cheek. "Are you sad?"

He managed to smile. "No. I am happy—happy to be here with you."

Acknowledgments

I wish to thank Asialink and ARTSA for the opportunity to research and write in Pakistan where I got the idea for *Mountain Wolf*. Thanks also to Murree Christian School, which was my host during most of the fellowhip and where I found recent research on the trafficking of children in Pakistan.

I wish to thank the following for their excellent help in the research and writing of *Mountain Wolf*: Sarmad Iqbal Khan, Programme Manager Advocacy & Urban Programmes, World Vision, Pakistan; Habib Ahmad, Advocacy Coordinator, World Vision, Pakistan; Matthew Stephens, Regional Anti-Trafficking Coordinator, World Vision, Middle East/Eastern Europe/Central Asia; Rebecca Lyman for help with research, contacts, and photographs; Frank Lyman for the firsthand information on Kala Dhaka and for reading the manuscript and giving it the thumbs up; Catch Tilly for reading an early draft and giving helpful suggestions. I am grateful for the inspiration gained from viewing photos of Kala Dhaka by Andy Goss and Frank Lyman.

Thank you to my agent, Jacinta di-Mase, and Lisa Berryman's wonderful team at HarperCollins, as well as Nicola O'Shea. I wish to thank those who have supported and helped me, especially in thinking of titles: my fellow eKIDnas at the SA Writers Centre, and my colleagues at Tabor Adelaide.

Resources that were helpful in writing *Mountain Wolf* include the following:

Asian Human Rights Commission, *Pakistan: the Cases of Missing Children Continue to Rise*, www.humanrights.asia, accessed 18 January 2011.

Bickerstaff, L, *Modern-Day Slavery*, Rosen Publishing Group, New York, 2010.

Child Prostitution in Pakistan, http://gvnet.com/childprostitution/Pakistan.htm

Child Protection and Welfare Bureau, www.cpwb.gov.pk/index.htm

ECPAT: End Child Prostitution, Child Pornography and Trafficking of Children for Sexual Purposes, www.ecpat.net

Jawadullah, "Health Hazards of Working on the Streets," *Discourse*, SPARC, Issue no 22, 2006.

Mortenson, G, *Three Cups of Tea*, Viking, New York, 2006.

Muhammad, T & Zafar, N, *Situational Analysis: Report on Prostitution of Boys in Pakistan (Lahore & Peshawar)*, ECPAT International in collaboration with Pakistan Pediatrics Association, 2006.

Pakistan Government, *Prevention and Control of Human Trafficking Ordinance*, 2002, www.protectionproject.org/wp-content/uploads/2010/09/Pakistan_TIP-Acts_2007.pdf

Saeed, F, *Taboo*, Oxford University Press, Karachi, 2002.

Tahir, Z, "Trafficking of Punjab's Children to Europe: The Case of France", *Discourse*, SPARC, Issue no 22, 2006.

Terminal Life: Pakistan's Street Working Children,
http://meero.worldvision.org/frontline-focus/
terminallife.html

World Vision, *Child Rescue,* www.meero.worldvision.org/
humantrafficking

About the Author

Rosanne Hawke is an award-winning Australian author. She has written more than twenty books for young people. Many of her books have been shortlisted or named as Notable Books in the Children's Book Council of Australia (CBCA) Awards. Rosanne has been a teacher and, for almost ten years, was an aid worker in Pakistan and the United Arab Emirates.